D1521400

The Rose by Another Name

Christopher Marlowe,
The Real Shakespeare

Melissa L. Olson

For Craig,
Who Always Believed.

Dear Reader,

The following presents the argument that Christopher Marlowe wrote the works of William Shakespeare. Who is Christopher Marlowe? It is reasonable you should ask. For four centuries the world has lauded William Shakespeare as one of the greatest writers of all time. His contemporary, Christopher Marlowe, the most popular and praised playwright of his time, has virtually disappeared from the world's consciousness. He certainly is not a household name, as is his famous peer. And yet, there is a growing body of evidence, and a large group of scholars, actors and laymen, who believe that Christopher Marlowe is the true author of the plays attributed to William Shakespeare.

Much has been written about the authorship debate, which has been going on for over two hundred years. Scholars and amateurs alike champion their candidates, from Oxford, to Bacon, even Queen Elizabeth. As the debate progresses, the Stratfordians (those who stand firmly behind William Shakespeare of Stratford-upon-Avon) have gone from laughing to scorn to angry rebuttal to simply, "Prove it." They have dug in their heels, no longer laughing, as more questions emerge which the orthodox view simply cannot answer: Where did William Shakespeare obtain his education, with his vast vocabulary, knowledge of the classics and insider's knowledge of the Queen's court? Where did Shakespeare get the money to buy an owner's share of the Globe Theater, when playwrights received a pittance for their work? Why didn't Shakespeare sue those who printed his plays without his consent, when he had a history of going to court over simple legal matters? Why are no books, manuscripts or documents of any kind listed in his very detailed will? Why do no original manuscripts of the plays exist? If there was a conspiracy to falsify the authorship of some of the best literary works ever written, why did it occur and how was the secret kept all these years?

Many find it impossible to reconcile William Shakespeare's life with the level of genius in his works. Moreover, genius is not enough to explain the plays and sonnets - the works demonstrate a level of education, exposure to foreign cultures, associations with members of the upper classes, and evidence of extreme personal conflict that William Shakespeare of Stratford-upon-Avon simply did not have the opportunity to experience. In short, the person who wrote these works had much more than genius – he had ability, experience, opportunity and motive. This story focuses on the life of one individual who had the ability, motive and opportunity to write some of the most wonderful literature the world has seen – poet, playwright, government agent, atheist, exile - Christopher Marlowe.

It may be impossible to prove that Christopher Marlowe wrote the Shakespeare canon, but the reader is encouraged to open his or her mind to the possibility. All excerpts at the beginning of each chapter are from historical documents – they are real, they actually exist. I urge the reader to pay close attention to these lines, as they provide the skeleton upon which I flesh out the story. Full transcripts of these historical documents can easily be found online. The characters in this story were real people as well. The narrative is mine.

Fiction based on fact – such stuff as dreams are made on.

Melissa L. Olson
Islesboro, Maine

Part I CANTERBURY 1564-1580

    The Beginning
    The King's Scholar
    The First Patron
    The Parker Scholar

Part II CAMBRIDGE 1580-1587

    The Poet
    The Recruitment
    The Queen's Agent
    The Go-Between
    The Portrait
    The Trap
    The Letter

Part III LONDON 1587-1593

    The Ascent
    The Circle
    The Machiavelli
    The Commission
    The Lowlands
    The Descent
    The Libel
    The Star Chamber
    The Betrayal
    The Arrest
    The Window
    The Nail
    The Retribution
    The Lamb
    The Death

The Inquest
The Escape
The Writ
The Pardon

Part IV EXILE 1593-1623

The Heir
The Continent
The Judgment
The Treasury
The Rival Poet
The Pilgrim
The Fury
The Reconciliation
The Darkness
The Sonnets
The Final Curtain
The Will
The Folio

EPILOGUE

Further Reading

Notes

The Players

The following were real people:

Edward Alleyn (1566-1626)
Lead actor of the Admiral's Men, who performed several of Christopher Marlowe's play in the new (1587) Rose Theatre.

Anthony Babington (1561-1586)
A wealthy young Catholic who plotted to assassinate Queen Elizabeth in order to place Mary Stuart on the English throne.

Anthony Bacon (1558-1601)
Older brother of writer and statesman Francis, nephew of William Cecil, Lord Burghley. Was a spy in France for Sir Francis Walsingham. Later came into the employ of Robert Devereux, earl of Essex.

Francis Bacon (1561-1626)
Brother of Anthony Bacon, nephew of Lord Burghley, statesman and lawyer, Francis acted as the earl of Essex's confidential advisor.

Richard Baines (dates unknown)
Ordained Catholic priest and double agent who wrote a list of accusations against Christopher Marlowe.

Edward Blount (1562-1632)
A well-respected publisher who produced works of both Christopher Marlowe and William Shakespeare.

Giordano Bruno (1548-1600)
Born of the Italian Renaissance, Bruno was a man of science, religion, philosophy, teaching and learning.

Richard Burbage (1568-1619)
Lead actor of the Lord Chamberlain's Men, which turned into the King's Men, the acting company that became synonymous with the plays of William Shakespeare.

Robert Cecil (c. 1563-1612)
Secretary of State after his father William's death in 1598, and James I's Secretary of State until Cecil's death in 1612, Robert Cecil was a master politician and instrumental in bringing James I to the English throne.

William Cecil, Lord Burghley (1520-1598)
Secretary of State, Lord High Treasurer, and chief advisor to Queen Elizabeth I.

Henry Chettle (c. 1564-c. 1606)
Published Robert Greene's *Groats-Worth of Witte*, a pamphlet denouncing the English theatre.

Richard Cholmeley (dates unknown)
Double agent, sometime servant of Robert Cecil, sometime of the earl of Essex.

Henry Condell (d. 1627) and John Heminges (d. 1630)
Fellow actors and theatrical partners of William Shakespeare who collected the plays attributed to Shakespeare and in 1623 had the manuscripts published as a folio. Both men were left money in William Shakespeare's will to buy mourning rings.

Ralph Crane (died c.1630)
Professional scrivener who worked for the King's Men and provided several manuscripts to be set into type for Shakespeare's Folio.

William Danby (b.1542)
Coroner of the Queen's Household who presided at the inquest into the death of Christopher Marlowe.

Robert Devereux, Earl of Essex (1565-1601)
Cousin of Queen Elizabeth I, ward of Lord Burghley, and son-in-law of Queen Elizabeth's spymaster Sir Francis Walsingham.

Thomas Drury (1551-1603)
Involved in the accusations of heresy, blasphemy and atheism against Marlowe and Cholmeley.

Richard Field (1561-1624)
Born in Stratford-upon-Avon, Field became the London printer of Shakespeare's first published poem "Venus and Adonis" in 1593.

Ingram Frizer (d. 1627)
Conman and servant of Thomas Walsingham. "Gentleman" accused of killing Christopher Marlowe in Deptford in May of 1593.

Gilbert Gifford (1560-?)
Double agent involved in the Babington Plot, which led to the execution of Mary Stuart.

Gifford Gilbert (dates unknown)
Goldsmith in the Lowlands who was involved in the coining dispute between Christopher Marlowe and Richard Baines.

Nicholas Goldsborough (dates unknown)
Headmaster of King's School in Canterbury during Christopher Marlowe's tenure.

Robert Greene (1558-1592)
Wrote *Greene's Groats-worth of Witte, bought with a million of Repentance* (published posthumously). Talented and successful as a playwright, Greene died penniless cursing the theatre.

Issac Jaggard (d. 1627)
Son of William Jaggard, who as a father and son team, published Shakespeare's Folio in 1623.

William Jaggard (c. 1568-1623)
Printer of questionable ethics who nevertheless was given the enormous task of printing Shakespeare's Folio.

Ben Jonson (1572-1637)
Popular playwright and contemporary of William Shakespeare and Christopher Marlowe.

Thomas Kyd (1558-1594)
Playwright, roommate and accuser of Marlowe as an atheist.

Niccolo Machiavelli (1469-1527)
Italian statesman who wrote *The Prince* in 1513.

Roger Manwood (1525-1592)
A lawyer from the Canterbury area, became Lord Chief
Baron of the Exchequer in 1578.

Christopher Marlowe (1564-?)
Son of a cobbler, recognized genius at an early age,
Marlowe earned scholarships and accolades throughout
his short life. Playwright, poet, spy, and atheist,
Christopher Marlowe was more likely to have written
the Shakespeare canon than William Shakespeare
himself.

Francis Meres (1565-1647)
Wrote a book that included literary criticism, being one
of the first to reflect on the works of William
Shakespeare. Somehow obtained knowledge of plays
and sonnets written by Shakespeare that were not yet
performed nor published.

Robert Norgate (d. 1587)
Master at Corpus Christi College, Cambridge, during
Marlowe's tenure.

Henry Percy, 9th Earl of Northumberland (1564-1632)
Known as the Wizard Earl, he was a Freethinker, who
spent time in the Tower.

John Parker (dates unknown)
Son of Matthew Parker, Archbishop of Canterbury
from 1559 to 1575. Charged with selecting students of
King's School in Canterbury for his father's scholarship
to Corpus Christi College at Cambridge.

John Penry (1559-1593)
A Puritan preacher from Wales, Penry printed tracts denouncing the Anglican Church, a capital offense.

Robert Poley (dates unknown)
Government agent who played a central role in uncovering the Babington Plot against Queen Elizabeth. Present at the scene of Christopher Marlowe's death.

Walter Ralegh (c. 1554-1618)
Writer, poet, soldier, politician, courtier, and explorer, this extraordinary man led a circle of Freethinkers, who questioned science and religion, to their own peril.

William Shakespeare (1564-1616)
Son of a glover, uneducated and unknown, William Shakespeare burst upon the English theatre world as an immensely talented poet, playwright and part owner of a leading players' company, but to this day scholars cannot match his works to his life.

Nicholas Skeres (b.1593)
Government agent present at the scene of Christopher Marlowe's death in Deptford.

Ferdinando Stanley, 5th Earl of Derby (1559-1594)
Also known as Lord Strange, the earl was a patron of the arts, especially theatre and playwrights.

Mary Stuart, Queen of Scots (1542-1587)
Catholic cousin of Protestant Queen Elizabeth I, Mary was once queen of France and queen of Scotland. Fled

to England and spent twenty years under her cousin's "protection."

Philip Sydney (1554-1586)
Soldier, poet, and brother of Robert Sidney, governor of the Lowlands. Died in battle and mourned as a national hero.

Robert Sydney (1563-1626)
Governor of the Lowlands, present-day Holland, brother of Philip Sydney.

Thomas Thorpe (c.1569-c. 1635)
Published Christopher Marlowe's *The First Book of Lucan* in 1600 and William Shakespeare's *Sonnets* in 1609. Strangely, there is no evidence that he owned either a print or bookshop.

Elizabeth Tudor, Queen Elizabeth I (1533-1603)
The Queen loved plays, and owed her life to Francis Walsingham's ring of spies.

Francis Walsingham (1532-1590)
Principal secretary to Queen Elizabeth I, known as her "spymaster." Related to Thomas Walsingham.

Thomas Walsingham (c.1561-1630)
Friend and patron of Christopher Marlowe, and fellow spy. First cousin once removed of Sir Francis Walsingham.

John Whitgift (c. 1530-1604)
Archbishop of Canterbury from 1583 to 1604. Became a privy councilor in 1586. Actively repressed

Catholicism and Puritanism, in the name of national security.

Henry Wriothesley, 3rd Earl of Southampton (1573-1624)
Another of Lord Burghley's wards, as was Robert Devereux, with whom Southampton forged a strong bond. Thought by many to be the subject of the "procreation" sonnets. William Shakespeare dedicated "Venus and Adonis" to him. Took part in the Essex Rebellion of 1601.

Part I
CANTERBURY
1564 – 1580

The Beginning
1564

The 26th day of ffebruary was Christened Christofer the sonne of John Marlow.

- Baptism record, St. George the Martyr Church, Canterbury, England

The great city bustled with importance. Its huge cathedral could be seen for miles.

Canterbury was an ancient city, settled by the Celts during the first hundred years after Christ's birth. The settlement was captured by the Romans, who built walls around the city in the third century AD to defend against attack from barbarians. The walls were rebuilt and reinforced with more towers in the fourteenth century. By the sixteenth century, the city walls consisted of six twin-towered gates and over twenty watchtowers. Canterbury was a well-defended city, attracting an influx of immigrants and travelers few European cities experienced.

Droves of people passed through the West Gate, a portal into the city that lay directly on the trade route between Dover and London. Soldiers, tradesmen, merchants, beggars – all came through Canterbury, either putting down roots in this prosperous city or continuing on to London and other English destinations to seek their fortunes. The city's proximity to the sea provided excellent positioning for commerce between England and the Continent, creating such wealth that Canterbury stood second only to London as an economic center.

Perhaps more importantly, Canterbury represented the heart of the English religion. The archbishop of Canterbury had been the head of the English Catholic Church since 672 AD. Since the martyrdom of Thomas a Becket in 1170, Canterbury Cathedral, built between c. 1100 and 1500, had welcomed multitudes of pilgrims every year. All Christendom journeyed to Canterbury to pay homage to Saint Thomas. English and foreign, rich and poor, educated and illiterate, low born and royalty – they came to Canterbury and left offerings in hope of a miracle or for the salvation of their soul, making the cathedral extremely wealthy. These pilgrimages inspired Chaucer to write his *Tales*.

The pilgrimages ended when Henry VIII dissolved the English monasteries in the late 1530s. He ended Catholic dominance over secular rule and made himself ruler not only of men's bodies, but of their souls as well. Becket's shrine was destroyed and the gold, silver and jewels, enough to fill three wagons, were carted off to London. Stories of the cathedral's loot spread far and wide, making the riches legendary.

The Catholic heyday was over, but Canterbury continued to serve as the center of the English Protestant Church. While the new religion ended the pilgrimages of Catholics, it started a flow of Protestant refugees from northern Europe, with thousands of French Huguenots and other European Protestants seeking refuge within the city walls. This influx of craftsmen and merchants caused commerce to boom, and Canterbury rose once again in wealth and prosperity. The Protestant immigrants enjoyed both religious and commercial tolerance under Queen Elizabeth I, who was determined to solidify the

Protestant faith within England. The archbishop of Canterbury continued to play an extremely important role not just in religion but in politics as well, and during Queen Elizabeth's reign enjoyed political importance second only to the queen.

London its only rival, Canterbury was the commercial, cultural, and spiritual hub of England. Born into this city, baptized on 26 February 1564 was Christopher Marlowe.

***

Two months later, in a small, densely illiterate village roughly sixty miles northwest of Canterbury, another child was born. William Shakespeare was christened on 26 April 1564 in Stratford-on-Avon. His parents John and Mary signed with their marks.

The King's Scholar
1573

Fifty poor boys, both destitute of the help of friends, and endowed with minds apt for learning, who shall be called scholars of the grammar school, and shall be sustained out of the funds of the Church.

- Statutes of the King's School (1541), chapter 27

Christopher fought his way to the front of the tight line that formed along the street. As did everyone else in the great city, Christopher wanted to see the Virgin Queen with his own eyes. The queen and her procession were making their way through the streets of Canterbury to the home of William Brooke, Lord Cobham, where her Majesty would keep court during her stay at Canterbury. She was honoring the city with her person on her fortieth birthday and would stay for two weeks. Archbishop Parker would be entertaining the queen at his palace that he had just renovated for the magnificent sum of fourteen hundred pounds!

After a wait that seemed an eternity, a roar went up and Queen Elizabeth came into view. She rode under a canopy carried by four of her knights. Her robes sparkled with jewels, which caught the sunlight and dazzled the crowd. At forty, she was still a beautiful woman, her red hair a blazing contrast to her white face. Christopher could understand why all her courtiers were in love with her, for he, too, fell in love with her that day.

After she passed, the crowd let out a collective breath. The people slowly dispersed and went back to tasks that had been put on hold in preparation for the

Queen's visit. Royalty had honored Canterbury before, but each visit brought a new excitement and reinforced its citizens' belief that it stood above all others as the greatest city in England.

Christopher was no exception. He had known for several years that, not only was his city special, but he himself was destined for greatness. He was aware at an early age of his supernatural power to attract attention and make things happen. Already people had noted his striking good looks, his beautiful singing voice and, above all, his intellect. Naturally, Christopher considered himself superior to his fellow class and playmates – and to a number of adults as well.

Perhaps he inherited this confidence from his father. John Marlowe was a well-established cobbler whose business boasted two apprentices and enabled him to employ a maid for his wife. Literate and ambitious, John took an active role in town affairs, acting as bondsman for couples wishing to marry, and pursuing his interests in court – suing and being sued. He had taught Christopher to read and write at an early age.

Among the crowds watching the queen were hundreds of immigrants – Canterbury abounded with them. Among Christopher's friends were French Huguenots, Protestant refugees from a very Catholic France. Only the year before, during August 1572, over two thousand Huguenots were killed in Paris during the St. Bartholomew Day Massacre. Many of those who survived made their way across the Channel to seek refuge in England. Elizabeth made it clear that she was an ally of anyone opposed to the pope. Many of these refugees made their homes in Canterbury and established businesses, taking advantage of the proximity to the river and access to London. Christopher had a sharp brain and a quick ear and easily picked up the language of his new neighbors.

When Christopher turned nine, his father enrolled him at the King's School. King's was the oldest and one of the best grammar schools in England, founded in the sixth century by Saint Augustine. In 1541 Henry VIII restructured the ancient Catholic school into a modern Protestant institution, providing education for fifty "destitute" boys who could not only read and write, but sing as well. In exchange for a place at the King's School, the students were expected to be choristers at the cathedral. Although mandated to serve the poor, the school often gave enrollment preference to sons of Kentish gentlemen, with commoners given a place only in the event of a vacancy. Christopher's acceptance at King's as a fee-paying commoner gave him the chance to rub elbows with the rich sons of landed gentry.

Because Christopher sang in the cathedral choir every morning, he had ample opportunity to view the queen during her two-week stay in Canterbury. The young boy felt enormous respect for his monarch and was filled with admiration for her beauty and power. He promised himself within the course of those two weeks that he would somehow devote his life to the queen, and he returned to his classes with renewed purpose and resolve.

Christopher excelled at the King's School. As a day student, he lived at home and arrived at school before the reading of the first psalm at 6 a.m. The lessons and readings were conducted in Latin, the only language the students were permitted to speak, even at play. Every morning the students broke fast together and attended High Mass, where Christopher sang with the other choristers.

One of the main functions of the King's School was to impart a thorough grounding in Latin grammar and speech, with a secondary emphasis on Greek. Lessons focused mainly on Latin grammar for the younger students and progressed to verse making, translation and oratory for the older students, with an emphasis on the classical masters. The lessons ended with a psalm at five in the afternoon, followed by dinner and an evening of study, where the younger students recited their lessons to the older students, after which Christopher would walk home.

Although the King's School charter made provisions for fifty scholarships, competition for those scholarships was high, and awarded only upon a vacancy. A vacancy might occur if a scholar did not meet the master's expectations and the school's standards. The headmaster conducted weekly examinations, at which time a scholarship could be taken from one student and given to another. It was in the best interests of a fee-paying commoner such as Christopher to exceed the school's expectations, particularly if he hoped to be awarded a coveted scholarship to one of England's finest grammar schools. The young Marlowe was therefore in almost constant competition with the other commoners and the weaker scholars.

To encourage fluency in the main topics of study, Latin and Greek, the scholars at the King's School performed plays in these languages at Christmastime. Once again, Christopher excelled. He was a natural performer, could remember his lines with little effort, and took an active role in directing his fellow players. Although the masters preferred morality plays that taught the students good behavior, Christopher encouraged his fellow classmates to perform less traditional plays that encouraged the audience to think for themselves. While his classmates resented his imperious attitude, they welcomed his help at translating the meaning of their lines, which aided in remembering and delivering them. Christopher enjoyed the playacting tremendously, but he enjoyed words more than actions. He liked the idea of putting words in people's mouths and watching the actors repeat the words on stage, in front of an appreciative audience. He made up his mind to give playwriting a try in the very near future.

***

There is no record of William Shakespeare attending grammar school in Stratford-on-Avon, nor anywhere else.

The First Patron
1576

Upon the death of the most honoured man, Sir Roger Manwood, Lord Chief Baron of the Queen's Exchequer. The terror of the night-prowler, harsh scourge of the profligate, both Jove's Alcides [Hercules] and vulture to the stubborn bandit, is buried within the funeral urn. Rejoice, you sons of crime. You the guiltless one, your hair unkempt on your sorrowful neck, mourn. The light of the courts, the glory of the venerable law is dead: Alas, with him to the exhausted shores of Acheron [the nether world] much virtue departed. Before one of so much worth, Envy, spare this man; be not too unwary of that which is in ashes, he whose look left so many thousands of mortals thunderstruck: Thus, though the bloodless messenger of Dis [death] shall wound you, may your bones rest happily, and your fame outlive the memorials of the marble tomb.

- Sir Roger Manwood's epitaph attributed to
Christopher Marlowe, December 1592.

When Christopher was twelve years old, his father John fell on hard times. Always ready for a fight, John found himself being sued for the grand sum of one hundred pounds. He could no longer afford to pay Christopher's tuition at the King's School, and there were no scholarships available at that time, so he decided to turn to the city's most prominent patron, Sir Roger Manwood.

Chief Baron of the Exchequer, Manwood held a high office in Her Majesty Queen Elizabeth's court, and therefore a high position in Canterbury. Although accused of oppression and corruption at court, Sir Roger proved a ready benefactor to Canterbury's needy.

A servant opened the door and ushered father and son into an impressive foyer. After a short wait, they were shown into Manwood's study where Sir Roger stood behind a massive desk. Sir Roger bid them be seated. The small group studied each other for a few moments. Christopher saw a lot more in Sir Roger than did his father. His father saw wealth. Christopher saw intelligence, ambition, greed... and danger.

Sir Roger began. "I believe you have a request to make of me?"

John licked his lips nervously, then said with bravado, "Yes, your lordship. You see, my boy here, Christopher, he's a smart lad. The top of his class at the King's School. The headmaster says so. Christopher started there when he was nine, me paying his fees as there were no scholarships. But you see, my lord, I have run into some financial difficulties that prevent me from paying his fees. So we've come to you, your lordship, to see if you can help us. It would be a shame to have him drop out of school, such a bright boy and all."

Manwood turned his cold eyes on Christopher. "So, my boy, you would like some of my money to stay in school. Why should I give it to you?"

John started to answer, but Sir Roger held up an imperious hand. "I want the boy to answer."

Christopher looked at Sir Roger and his brown eyes glittered. He could tell instantly what sort of man he was dealing with. "Your lordship, I would be very grateful for your patronage. You see, I am a poor boy, but I work hard to learn my Latin and my grammar. My family is counting on me to become a clergyman when I become older, to make them proud and serve the

Church. I must stay in school. Please, my lord, won't you help me?"

John stared at his son. He had never heard Christopher speak this way in his life. Christopher had a sharp tongue and quick wit that he used on a regular basis with his four younger sisters, his classmates, and even on occasion, his parents, although he had felt the back of his father's hand more than once because of it. Christopher was not one to speak in such a deferential tone. But John kept quiet.

Manwood remained impassive. "I assume you can read and write, and know your Latin grammar. And you sing as well?"

"Yes, your lordship. I sang for the queen on her fortieth birthday. She is very beautiful and I love her with all my heart."

"Yes, well, be that as it may, I need to know that you will continue to do well at King's School, if you are to be the recipient of my patronage. If you do not do well, I will withdraw my support. I will agree to this arrangement for the time being, but I expect full reports each year from the headmaster on your progress. And, of course, I expect payment in return." John started, but Sir Roger waved him silent. "Not from you, from the boy here. I expect great things from him, as my beneficiary. He will, no doubt, repay me in some way in the future. Just how I haven't decided, but there is time."

Christopher sprang to his feet, hands clasped. "Oh, thank you, your lordship, thank you for your generosity. If ever I can serve you, it would be my pleasure and my honor to repay you for your kindness. I can never thank you enough. Just tell me when and how I can repay you and I'll do it, on my knees…"

11

John led his son out of the room somewhat hastily. Out on the street he gave his son a cuff. "What the devil were you playing at? Going on like that. You looked a proper fool."

"Father, Sir Roger wanted me to look a proper fool. He enjoys the power. We got the money, didn't we?"

"That's so, my boy, that's so. Don't you ever let anybody think they're smarter or better than you. You are John Marlowe's son, and that's something to be proud of."

"Yes, Father, I agree. There are few people in this world who are better or smarter than I, and I have yet to meet one of them."

John laughed. That was the Christopher he knew. They hurried down the street to tell the family their news.

After a further two years as a fee-paying commoner, Christopher was finally awarded a scholarship in the winter of 1578, demonstrating his scholastic achievement at the King's School and underscoring the academic disgrace of John Emley, the former holder of the scholarship. Christopher had outperformed all the other commoners to win this prize, no easy task in the intense atmosphere of constant competition. The awarding of this scholarship relieved Sir Roger of future payment. However, neither he nor Christopher ever forgot the boy's debt.[1]

---

[1]Marlowe had further reason to thank Roger Manwood. In 1589, Christopher and his fellow playwright Tom Watson were arrested for the death of William Bradley, whom Watson killed in a street fight. Manwood was the judge and acquitted them both on grounds of self-defense.

The Parker Scholar
Spring 1580

All which schollers shall and must at the time of their election be so entred into the skill of song as that they shall at first sight solf and sing plaine song. And that they shalbe of the best and aptest schollers well instructed in their gramer and if it may be such as can make a verse.

- Terms of the Parker Scholarship to Corpus Christ College, Cambridge University, 1541

John Parker paid a visit to King's School. He was the son of the esteemed Dr. Matthew Parker, late archbishop of Canterbury who had died five years previously. Mathew Parker had also been master of Corpus Christi College at Cambridge between 1544 and 1553, and in his will had made provisions of several scholarships for worthy young men to attend Corpus Christi. One of the scholarships was to go to a native of Canterbury who attended the King's School. Hence, John Parker's visit. The younger Parker was to interview masters and students to determine who would receive this coveted scholarship.

The headmaster greeted Parker at the door of his chambers. As they both settled into chairs, Parker came directly to the point. "Master Goldsborough, as you know, I have come here to find a boy who is worthy of receiving my late father's generous scholarship to attend Corpus Christi. The terms of the scholarship are that the boy must be in financial need, must be able to compose a Latin verse, must possess a strong singing voice, and must be able to sight read and sing. He will be required to participate in the college choir during his tenure. Upon graduation, the scholar is expected to enter holy orders, which will repay his debt to my father and serve the Church. And, of course, we have only the brightest students at Corpus Christi and therefore require a student of exceptional abilities in all his studies. Do you have a student of this caliber attending the King's School at this time?"

Goldsborough remained silent. Of course, Christopher Marlowe sprang to mind, but he hesitated to recommend him to Parker. While Goldsborough recognized Christopher's brilliant mind, he also knew of Marlowe's arrogance towards his fellow classmates and the masters who taught him. Arrogance had caused the ruin of many a man – men who began with far more than Christopher Marlowe. Wealthy men, men of aristocracy, men of nobility. Marlowe possessed this arrogance, even though he had been born into nothing. Goldsborough wondered how Marlowe would handle his arrogance, and his intelligence. While Goldsborough admired Christopher's brilliance, he disliked the boy's conceit.

Parker waited patiently. He knew this was an important decision, one he appreciated Goldsborough taking seriously. Finally Goldsborough spoke. "I do know of such a student. A brilliant boy, the likes of which we have not seen at the King's School for a very long time. His name is Christopher Marlowe, here on scholarship. His father is a cobbler and sometimes town official. A self-important, annoying little man. For some time, Sir Roger Manwood paid Marlowe's tuition, but two years ago the school awarded the boy a scholarship on his own merit. He performs extremely well in all his studies, especially translating Latin, and has even written his own verses." Goldsborough hesitated.

14

"However, he is a difficult personality. He is a leader among the other boys here. They both fear and respect him. And the masters have often been caught out by his wit. Somehow, though, he usually escapes punishment."

John Parker was intrigued. "I would like to meet this boy. We want only the keenest minds at Corpus Christi. We have ways of disciplining temperament."

"Very well, I will call him in." Goldsborough went to the door where an attendant stood waiting. "Please fetch Christopher Marlowe to my chambers at once."

The two men had only a few minutes to wait. Christopher knew of Parker's visit and naturally assumed he would be called in to meet him. He had spent the morning in close proximity to Goldsborough's chambers.

Christopher entered the room and bowed first to Master Goldsborough and then to John Parker. Goldsborough spoke, "Marlowe, I assume you know why I have called you here. This is John Parker, son of Archbishop Parker, God rest his soul. Mr. Parker has asked me to recommend a King's boy to receive one of his father's scholarships to Corpus Christi. I am considering recommending you."

Christopher listened to this news impassively. He turned to look at Parker, and the two studied each other. Parker finally spoke, "Well, young Marlowe, what have you to say for yourself? Do you feel you deserve my father's scholarship?"

A dangerous light flickered in Christopher's eye, but he extinguished it before Parker could recognize it (Goldsborough, however, did not miss the look). Again, Christopher bowed, "Please, your honor, I would be very honored to receive your worthy father's charity. I am at the top of my class in all subjects."

Parker wasn't sure if he caught a superior tone in Christopher's reply, so he let it pass. "As you know, exceptional singing skills are required of the scholarship recipient. I have brought some sheet music that I would like you to study and be prepared to sing for me within the hour." He handed the sheets to Christopher.

Christopher glanced over the sheets. "If you please, your honor, an hour will not be necessary. I can sing this for you now."

Parker looked startled. Goldsborough looked amused. He had no doubt Christopher would perform the piece perfectly.

When Christopher finished, quietness settled in the room. Finally, Parker stirred and said, "That was very good, very good indeed. We could use a fine voice like that in the choir. Now, if you would study these texts in Latin and translate them. Again, I will give you one hour to complete the task. I doubt you will find this exercise as easy as the first."

Again, he handed some sheets to Christopher, who glanced over them quickly. "You are right, your honor, I will need more time on this exercise." Goldsborough showed him to a desk overlooking the yard and Christopher began to write. His hand flew over the page. Parker watched him for a few moments and turned to begin a conversation with the headmaster. The two men spoke no more than ten minutes before Christopher stood and came over to their chairs, holding out the transcribed document.

"Please, your honor, I have finished." Again, was the tone mocking? Parker looked quickly at Christopher, whose face was blank. He looked at the paper in front of him. It was perfect, no errors and no mark outs. It was the most precise, most elegant translation of this text Parker had ever seen (including his own). He remained quiet for a few moments, then turned to Goldsborough. "I have found my scholarship recipient. Christopher Marlowe is accepted into Corpus Christi College as a Parker Scholar. He is to present himself to the college the third week of September to begin his studies. I have no doubt he will make an excellent addition to our esteemed college." He rose and bowed to Goldsborough. Then he turned to Christopher, "Congratulations, young man, I trust you shall honor our school." Christopher bowed and said, "Thank you, your honor, I trust that I shall." They looked each other in the eye for a long moment, then John Parker left the room and returned to Cambridge.

Part II
CAMBRIDGE
1580 – 1587

The Poet
1582

How apt her breasts were to be prest by me.
How smooth a belly under her wast saw I,
How large a legge, and what a lustie thigh?
To leave the rest, all liked me passing well,
I clinged her naked body, downe she fell,
Judge you the rest, being tirde she bad me kiss;
Jove send me more such after-noones as this.

- Christopher Marlowe's translation of
"Corinnae concubitus." Ovid's *Elegia 5*

Christopher kept busy at Corpus Christi
College. Although the academic day was even more
demanding than at the King's School, Christopher
found time to set for himself several tasks that were to
influence his future and set the course of his life. He
began to write plays.

His first dramatic work, *The True History of George
Scanderbeg*, concerned the heroic Christian prince of
Albania who fought and defeated the infidel Turks and
drove them from his homeland. Christopher had
become fascinated with Scanderbeg's life during his
studies. The prince was courageous, chivalrous, and
possessed a warlike prowess that Christopher admired
very much. In fact, Christopher perceived many of the
same qualities in himself.

Christopher then turned to poetry. He wanted
to try his hand at blank verse, newly introduced to
England from Italy, where it was widely used because it
resembled classical, unrhymed poetry. For practice, he

selected the first book of Lucan's *Pharsalia*, a epic poem about the civil war between Caesar and Pompey.

Blank verse comprises unrhymed lines all using the same meter. Christopher preferred iambic pentameter, which gave him great range and flexibility. He found the form delightful to work with, and astounded his masters with his skill. Never before had they encountered a student of such genius. The masters of Corpus Christi were used to students struggling to translate works verbatim, not transform them into beautiful English poetry. But that is exactly what Christopher did.

His next work he did not make known to the masters. Christopher translated Ovid's *Elegies*, a collection of erotic love poems to a mistress. Ovid, a Roman poet who lived during the time of Christ, lived in exile because of the sexual content of these poems, and the poems were not considered any more respectable in sixteeen century Protestant England. Christopher greatly admired the classical poet's style of writing and use of language. Again, he used blank verse and translated Ovid's rhyming couplets into iambic pentameter. The poems caused a quiet sensation at Corpus, with students reading them in secret from the ever-watchful masters.

One day, John Walford, a fellow student at Corpus, came upon Christopher at his desk, writing furiously upon a piece of well-worn paper. "How now, my friend, what are you working on so seriously? Don't tell me you are translating more Ovid for us. The fellows can't take much more temptation."

Christopher looked up. "No, I am working on a play. I'm calling it *Dido, Queen of Carthage*, using Virgil's *Aeneid* as inspiration. Queen Dido falls in love with

Aeneas but he leaves her and goes to Rome. Then she kills herself."

"Well, when do we get to see this masterpiece? Who will be performing it?"

"I am writing it for Her Majesty's Children of the Chapel. There are some delicious scenes between gods and children that I just couldn't resist."

"Are the masters going to approve of such scenes?"

"Well, they can hardly object. It's based on classical literature. Besides, it's only a brief scene between Jupiter and Ganymede that will cause a stir. But then, the gods were known to be promiscuous, with adults and children alike."

"Wonderful. I can't wait to see it. But don't you ever worry about your studies? I can hardly keep up."

"No, my friend, I don't worry about such things. The masters don't know it yet but I have no intention of entering holy orders. I have known for quite a while the Church is not my calling."

"What is your calling?"

"An excellent question; however I do not know the full answer. But I know it involves playwriting. It makes me feel alive like nothing else in the world. I have no doubt that I was born to write, I live to write, I am nothing without writing. The words, the lines, the poems, the plays! They are my world, the essence of my being. Without words I am nothing."

John stared at him. "I had no idea you had been affected so. We have enjoyed your Ovid, and I know that no one else could have translated the works as beautifully as you, but I did not know how much they moved you."

"Yes, poetry and plays move me. I would write plays that move others as well, that show the beauty of the English language, and of course my skill. Mark my words, my friend, the world has never seen the likes of me, and I will be remembered for all eternity."

"Of that, my friend, I have no doubt, no doubt at all."

The boy actors of the Chapel staged the first performance of *Dido*. The audience found the English blank verse of the play refreshing after the Latin and Greeks plays performed for so many years. The fellows of Corpus, confounded by an intellect superior to their own, acknowledged Christopher's immense talent. Never had they encountered a mind such as his within the walls of the venerated college.

***

Back in Stratford, as Christopher Marlowe was translating erotic Greek poetry by Ovid, the most influential classical poet in the Shakespeare canon, and writing his first plays, William Shakespeare married Anne Hathaway, a woman eight years his elder. Six months later their first child Susanna was born.

The Recruitment
1584

Navarre, give me thy hand. I here do swear
To ruinate that wicked church of Rome,
That hatcheth up such bloody practices,
And here protest eternal love to thee,
And to the Queen of England specially,
Whom God hath blest for hating papistry.

- Christopher Marlowe, *Massacre at Paris*

The day after he received his bachelor of arts degree, Christopher was summoned into Dr. Norgate's chambers. Norgate, headmaster of Corpus Christi College, was deemed incompetent by most of the fellows and students. When Christopher arrived, he found Norgate with a stranger introduced to Christopher as none other than Sir Francis Walsingham, Queen Elizabeth's secretary of state and head of her spy network.

When the introductions were over, Mr. Secretary Walsingham turned to Norgate and said, "I would speak with young Marlowe here in private, if you would be so kind." Norgate looked taken aback but made no objection and withdrew, leaving Walsingham and Marlowe regarding each other. The secretary spoke first. "I have come to enlist you into Her Majesty's service." He paused to see Christopher's reaction, but saw none. He continued, "As you know, Lord Burghley, Her Majesty's Lord Treasurer, is chancellor of Cambridge University. He has advisors here at Corpus on the lookout for promising young men. The advisors tell me you have the makings of an excellent servant to the crown. According to your masters, you are extremely intelligent (although your marks don't always reflect this – they say you don't apply yourself), are fluent in French, are a leader among your classmates, have a prodigious memory and an eye for detail." Again he paused. "The question is do you have the ability to read people who have something to hide? Can you tell the difference between the truth and a lie? Can you make people believe in you, when you are lying to them? And, most important, do you swear allegiance to the queen above all others? Those are the qualities that will make you an invaluable government agent, and those are the qualities that will keep you alive."

Christopher eyed the secretary silently. He knew instinctively that he was already involved with Her Majesty's spy network, having been selected by Burghley's men as a promising agent. To refuse was not an option. There had been rumors among the scholars that Corpus supplied agents for Her Majesty's secret service but of course this was never confirmed or spoken of. Now confirmation was sitting right in front of him.

Before Christopher could respond, Walsingham continued. "Of course, you will be compensated for your services. I know that scholars here at Corpus don't enjoy many comforts. A little extra money would come in handy, I don't doubt." He eyed Christopher's worn robes and old shoes.

Christopher's eyes narrowed and for the first time he displayed some emotion. "Your honor, I would gladly give my life in the service of my queen, with no thought of material gain. However, if I am expected to travel to France, I would need to cover my expenses, which may be considerable."

Walsingham's own eyes narrowed and he asked, "Why did you mention France? I never spoke of France."

Christopher calmly replied, "Because Mary Stuart must be in communication with her supporters in France and she poses a serious threat to the English throne; because France is in the midst of religious turmoil that threatens our own country's security; and because, as you have already pointed out, I speak French as if I had been born there. Where else would I be going in Her Majesty's service?"

Mr. Secretary Walsingham permitted himself a small smile. "I see Lord Burghley's advisors were right. They have chosen well." He stood, and so did Christopher. "I have arranged for you to meet a relative of mine, Thomas Walsingham. He is of your age but has been in my service for several years now and will serve as your trainer. Pay close attention to what he has to say. It will serve you well."

The Queen's Agent
London

Not mine own fears, nor the prophetic soul
Of the wide world dreaming on things to come,
Can yet the lease of my true love control,
Supposed as forfeit to a confined doom.

- William Shakespeare. Sonnet 107

The city seethed with life, and with the possibility of death. Never had Christopher felt these dangerous extremes more sharply than on his first visit to the capitol to meet Thomas Walsingham. Christopher had skirted London when he first traveled to Cambridge, upon the advice of John Parker who warned against the many distractions of the city. As an undergraduate of Corpus Christi College, Christopher had not been permitted to leave college grounds. But as a new agent employed by none other than Sir Francis himself, Christopher enjoyed a sense of freedom he had never before experienced. He liked it. It made him feel powerful and dangerous, not to be trifled with. Far too long he had endured the mundane masters and foolish undergraduates of Corpus. Now he was a man with important work to do, to save queen and country from those who wished to destroy both. Yes, Christopher felt very powerful.

Upon entering London, Christopher found his way to Seething Street, home of Mr. Secretary Walsingham and the rooms of the secretary's cousin. Thomas Walsingham, Christopher discovered, held a prominent position in Her Majesty's spy network, having performed sensitive and important tasks, such as accompanying Sir Francis to France during marriage negotiations between Queen Elizabeth and the French king's brother Francois, duc d'Anjou, which ultimately failed.

A servant opened the door and showed Christopher into Thomas Walsingham's chambers. Christopher bowed, then took the seat offered. Walsingham smiled engagingly. "So, you've decided to join forces to protect the queen from enemies both foreign and domestic, eh? This job is challenging as well as rewarding. How rewarding and how challenging you will find out soon enough." Christopher remained silent.

Walsingham studied Christopher for a few moments. "I can see you are a man of few words, one who knows how to gather information while keeping his mouth shut. That trait will serve you well in this business. May even save your life. What have you learned so far?"

Christopher continued to regard Walsingham silently. Then he began to speak. "Sir, I have learned a great many things. First, you are not as you seem. You have many secrets that you share with no one, because you trust no one. Second, men would be wise not to put their trust in you, because you seek to deceive. And third, men would be wise to stay in your graces, because you can be a powerful ally, as well as a dangerous enemy."

Thomas Walsingham raised his eyebrows. "You are very perceptive. Remarkably so, since we have only just met. I *am* a good friend, and a dangerous enemy. And in our line of work, we can not be too careful whom we trust with our secrets. Better to trust no one than one too many."

"Sir, I hope that one day you will be able to put your trust in me. I am a man of my word, and I have sworn, upon my life, to protect the queen from those who wish to see her fall."

"Well said. But if we are to be working together, you must call me Thomas. The queen needs men like you. But as you will see, it is difficult to know who is true and who is false in this business. I look forward to putting my trust in you, Christopher, as I hope you will learn that you can put your trust in me."

The two men spent the day in deep conversation. Thomas revealed Christopher's first assignment, one that almost took Christopher's breath away. He was to go to France, to Rheims. At the seminary, where many anti-Protestant conspiracies against Elizabeth had hatched, Christopher was to pose as a Catholic convert and find a likely candidate who would become a double agent for the queen.

"You see, Christopher, we need an agent in Rheims, a Catholic who will give us information about plots against the queen. Your task is to find that person. Use whatever methods necessary. Bribery, blackmail – both have worked well in the past. This person will be in danger, and his loyalties will always be suspect. Never turn your back. Your goal is to live to serve another day."

Christopher replied reflectively, "Yes, I believe I will survive, in one form or another. Time will tell."

The Go-Between
1584-1585
Rheims, France

Freely give unto this young scholar that hath been long studying at Rheims; as cunning in Greek, Latin and other languages, as the other in music and mathematics.

- William Shakespeare. *The Taming of the Shrew*

So Christopher set forth to France, to the Catholic seminary in Rheims, under the auspices of the English College at Douai, to unearth a double agent. He spent over a year and a half convincing the priests and novitiates that he was a Catholic who wanted to help them in their cause to overthrow Protestant Elizabeth and place Catholic Mary, queen of Scots, on the English throne. He traveled back and forth between Rheims and Corpus Christi, where his absences were duly recorded. Christopher needed to find a man that he could turn. He found that man in Gilbert Gifford.

Born in Staffordshire in 1560, Gifford came from a recusant Catholic family (his father John paid fines for not attending Protestant services). Gifford entered the Catholic seminary in France when he was seventeen, but he was expelled, for reasons kept within the walls of the seminary. In 1582 Cardinal Allen gave him a second chance, but Gifford still could not settle to religious life. He left first for England, then France, then Rome. Allen gave him a third chance in 1583, and Gifford was finally ordained as a deacon in 1585.

As his record attests, Gifford had conflicting feelings about his Catholic faith. It was this conflict that caused Christopher to target him as a potential double agent. Gifford had gone to Paris to meet with John Savage and Thomas Morgan, agents of Queen Mary of Scots, ostensibly to plot Queen Elizabeth's assassination. Christopher knew of these meetings, and also of Gifford's past history in and out of the seminary. He laid his trap.

In December 1585, Gifford planned a trip to London. Christopher made these plans known to Mr. Secretary Walsingham, and upon his arrival, Gifford was detained and brought before the spymaster.

Gifford was escorted into Mr. Secretary's chambers by two guards. He was startled to see Marlowe, whom he had last seen in Rheims and knew only as a young English zealot with a passionate hatred for Protestantism in general and Queen Elizabeth in particular. Why was he sitting in the office of the queen's spymaster? Gifford's fear grew.

Walsingham turned to the guards and dismissed them. He graciously offered Gifford a seat. Gifford slowly sat down and looked at Marlowe warily. Christopher's face showed no emotion.

Mr. Secretary Walsingham spoke, "Mr. Gifford, do you know why you are here?" Gifford licked his lips and shook his head. He attempted bravado. "No, your honor, I am much offended. I have done nothing wrong, and my business in London has been disrupted."

"And what business is that, sir?"

"I would not say, your honor. It is a private matter."

"But, sir, there *are* no private matters in England, especially when it comes to the safety of the queen. You will answer me, if you want to live. You see, Marlowe here, whom I believe you know from Rheims, is actually working on her Majesty's behalf. He has learned a great deal of interesting information about your dealings in Paris, where I understand you met with certain persons who, shall we say, do not act in the best interest of her Majesty, but in the interests of her rival Mary Stuart." He put up a hand as Gifford began to rise from his chair in protest. "There is no use denying this information. You have been followed for over six months, and I have found Marlowe's reports quite reliable. You, on the other hand, have not proved so reliable. In and out of the seminary, sometimes of your own accord, sometimes not. I wonder where your loyalties really lie, as must Cardinal Allen. If he ever found out you were in our chambers, discussing matters behind closed doors, your life would no doubt be in peril, even from a devout man such as the cardinal. "

Gifford blanched. He knew his actions would look suspicious, especially when embellished by that snake Marlowe. He decided to cooperate, for the time being.

"Well, your honor, what would you have me do? I am but a poor deacon of the Catholic Church, simply wishing to practice my faith unmolested. But if it is God's will for me to serve the queen, I will do my best."

"I don't doubt. This is what you must do. You will return to your native Staffordshire, where Mary Stuart is being held in Chartley Hall, with Sir Amias Paulet as her "host," shall we say. You will gain her confidence and offer to help her raise aid in France. You will act as her agent and transport messages between her and her supporters. But you will, of course, make sure that I see those messages first. We will devise a method that you will follow. And, of course, Marlowe here will be watching your every move to make sure that you stay on the right side of this battle."

Gilbert Gifford looked from Secretary Walsingham to Christopher, who remained silent but watched him with uncannily shrewd eyes. This reaffirmed his decision to cooperate. "Very well, your honor, I see that I must obey. But how am I to establish a relationship with Queen Mary, or gain her trust?"

"Ah, do not fear, Marlowe will be able to assist you in making the right acquaintances. He is a man of many talents." Christopher bowed his head modestly, but didn't fail to see Gifford's look of hatred. "Marlowe will act as your contact both here in England and at Rheims. You will deliver any and all messages to him, and he will see that they get into my hands. And do not," here he turned his piercing gaze full upon Gifford, "for one instant, forget that if you betray her Majesty, your end will be guaranteed. The queen tolerates no treason, and is willing to make an example of those who betray her. Do not test her, nor me."

Secretary Walsingham called the guards in and instructed them to escort Gifford back to the ship that was leaving for France. "You and Marlowe will make your plans in Rheims. You will return to England once those plans are completed. Until then, take care that you do not betray the queen. We will be watching."

With a final backward glance, Gifford left. Secretary Walsingham turned to Christopher. "Well, Marlowe, I believe you have selected well. Gilbert Gifford has much to offer and much to lose. I have no doubt he will prove very useful. Watch him closely."

"I will, Mr. Secretary. I have found him to be foolish and weak, easily manipulated but impossible to trust. He will serve our purpose, but not for too long."

The Portrait
1585

Consum'd with that which it was nourish'd by.

- William Shakespeare, Sonnet 73

Christopher had spent the better part of his fifth and sixth college years in France, a fact that did not sit well with Master Norgate. Christopher's scholarship payments of a shilling per week were withheld during his absences from Corpus Christi, duly recorded in the college's buttery books. This did not daunt Christopher in the least. Not only did he receive payment from Mr. Secretary Francis Walsingham, but his accounts at the buttery were being paid as well. He could well afford to treat himself and his friends to an evening of enjoyment at the government's expense, which he did.

On one of his trips to London, his fellow agent and now friend Thomas Walsingham made an intriguing proposition. "You know, Christopher, a man in your position should have his portrait painted."

Christopher laughed. "And what, pray tell, is my position?"

"Well, you have a bachelor's degree from Cambridge University and are now pursuing your master's degree from that esteemed seat of learning, you are in the service of the queen of England, and you have me, Thomas Walsingham, cousin to Sir Francis Walsingham, secretary of state and spymaster for her Majesty, for a friend. I believe you should declare your position to the world, for all to see."

Christopher pondered the idea for a while. He liked it. Why shouldn't he have his portrait painted? Others lower than he had their likenesses painted. Thomas was right. Christopher had a lot of which to be proud, and he did want the world to know of his success. "Yes, Thomas, I believe you are right, I should have my portrait painted. But what about the little details, like who should paint it, and how much it will cost?'

Thomas waved his hand. "Oh, leave all that to me. I will take care of everything. You just show up when you are told and all will be well."

"Thank you, Thomas, I appreciate your generosity, as always. I wonder if I shall ever be able to repay the kindness you have shown me, and your friendship. Both mean a great deal to me, not to mention the excellent training you have provided me. I have seen more these past few months then most men see in a lifetime."

Thomas smiled. "Be here next Monday. I will have a painter ready for you. I will also find something suitable for you to wear. You can't be remembered in those awful college robes, which show not one wit of your personality."

The following Monday, Christopher arrived at Thomas's chambers at the prescribed time. When he entered, he was introduced to the artist, a small Spaniard. Over a chair hung a doublet, the most beautiful, most expensive doublet Christopher had ever laid eyes on. "What is this? You can't be serious. You expect me to wear this for my portrait? You know I am not allowed to wear such a garment – it is too rich for a lowly university scholar. Where did you get it?"

Thomas laughed. "Never mind where I got it. Isn't it handsome? It suits you perfectly. Bold, colorful, successful – primed to conquer the world. For that is what you are going to do, Christopher, mark my words. I have seen brilliance in you. Once I come into my inheritance I will become your patron. I want you to make us both famous, for history to record. You and I make a fine team – my position, your intellect. Yes, Christopher, you must wear the doublet. This portrait is for posterity, for future generations to understand that you are a man of importance. I will keep the portrait here in my chambers until you are graduated. Then perhaps you can present it to Master Norgate, whom I believe is not your strongest supporter at Corpus? He who has been hounding you for your absences from college? How foolish he would feel if he were to know the truth."

Christopher eyed the doublet doubtfully, then put it on. He felt the rich fabric and the silk underneath, showing through the slashed velvet. He felt the weight of the buttons. "The doublet is fine, wonderful in fact. But what of the collar? It is not as fashionable as the ruff."

"I though the simple collar of cobweb lawn suits you better – shows you are a scholar and an intellect, not a court dandy like myself."

Christopher nodded. He loved the idea of having his portrait painted, and yet, there was still a niggling feeling in his mind, a feeling of unease, almost fear, that he couldn't shake. Of course it must have to do with the dangers associated with his line of work. Carelessness and stupidity had cost men their lives. Christopher was neither careless nor stupid. "Shall we begin?"

And so Christopher sat, day after day for the better part of the week, until the painter declared the work finished. Christopher stood and came around to the easel. He saw a very good likeness of himself, showing his sardonic gaze, his flamboyant hairstyle that irked the college officials no end, and the outrageous doublet that was sure to send his masters into a rage. Christopher had insisted on crossing his arms for the portrait, a posture that made the artist unhappy. "But it looks as if you are hiding something."

"Perhaps I am," was all Christopher said.

Thomas was delighted with the portrait. "It reflects you perfectly. I will have it framed as a panel, to be included at the Masters' Lodge at Corpus when they receive it. After all, time will show that you are to be one of the college's most famous sons. But for now I will have the pleasure of your likeness with me for a while."

Christopher looked at the painting again. "It is missing something." The artist had dated the painting, 1585, in the upper left-hand corner, and included Christopher's age, twenty-one. "I would like to include the words "Quod me nutruit me destruit."

"'That which nourishes me destroys me?' Whatever do you mean, my dear boy?"

"Just that I can't shake this feeling of doom, that this path I am on will lead to my destruction. Serving the queen has been profitable, in more ways than one, but I can't help feeling that it will be the end of me, somehow."

"Nonsense. You must simply be careful. You are smarter than any of them out there. You will be fine."

"Perhaps you are right." Christopher gazed at the portrait while the artist added the inscription. But he thought to himself, "Perhaps not." [2]

***

Back in Stratford, life was quiet. The only event of note from the Shakespeare household was the birth of twins, Judith and Hamnet, born in February of 1585.

---

[2] In 1953, two panels of a portrait as described above were discovered among the debris of the Master's Lodge at Corpus Christi College, which was being renovated for the new master. The panels were restored and now hang again on the walls of Corpus Christi, identified as the only likeness in existence of Christopher Marlowe.

The Trap
1586

To this I witness call the fools of Time,
Which die for goodness, who have liv'd for crime.

- William Shakespeare, Sonnet 124

Gilbert Gifford quickly established a trusting relationship with Mary Stuart, given his connections to Staffordshire and Christopher's behind-the-scenes maneuvering. Mary trusted Gilbert completely, because her options were running out.

Daughter of King James V of Scotland and Mary of Guise, France, Mary Stuart became queen of Scotland upon her father's death on 14 December 1542 when she was just six days old. Because of political and religious turmoil in Scotland, her mother sent Mary to France when she was five years old. Her primary language, therefore, was French, and her religion Catholic. She was betrothed to and married Francois, dauphin of France in 1558 when she was sixteen and he fourteen. Mary became queen of two countries when Francois ascended the French throne in 1559. Francois died in 1560, and because French law decreed that a woman could not be sole monarch of the French throne, Mary returned to Scotland to resume the Scottish throne. She remarried twice, both with disastrous results, and managed to antagonize much of Protestant Scotland by overtly practicing her Catholic faith.

Forced to abdicate the Scottish throne, Mary fled to England in July of 1567 to seek the protection of her cousin Queen Elizabeth. Her claim, however, to

41

the English throne was too close for comfort. As the granddaughter of Henry VIII's sister Margaret Tudor, who had married King James IV of Scotland, Mary represented a legitimate rival to her cousin Elizabeth, whose Protestant supporters had no intention of letting Catholic Mary get her hands on the English throne. Mary was therefore placed under Elizabeth's "protection," which was, in fact, house arrest. She was not permitted to travel unattended, leave the country or have certain visitors, and her every move was monitored.

Imprisoned by her cousin for nearly twenty years, Mary was almost beyond hope of release and was ready to grasp any straw offered. Gilbert Gifford offered a straw. He would carry messages for her to France, to increase support and possibly set up a means of escape. He posed as a merchant, the messages hidden in beer barrels. Gifford, acting as a double agent, would deliver the barrels to London, where the messages would be removed, decoded by Thomas Phelippes, Mr. Secretary Walsingham's code breaker, returned to the barrels and in due course delivered to the intended hands in France. Gifford himself accompanied the barrels to France, where he hand-delivered Mary's messages to the French court.

Christopher watched Gifford closely. His instinctive suspicion of Gifford proved accurate. Christopher felt certain that given the slightest opportunity, Gifford would switch sides or flee and Elizabeth could not afford to have him do either. The noose was tightening on Mary and Elizabeth's supporters wanted her removed, once and for all.

Eventually, the trap worked. Mary implicated herself, as well as a young Catholic aristocrat by the name of Anthony Babington and several other conspirators who were plotting to assassinate Elizabeth and place Catholic Mary Stuart on the English throne. Sir Francis finally had the proof he needed – a letter signed by Mary to Babington giving permission to use bodily force against Elizabeth in order to gain Mary's freedom.

When Gifford learned that the trap was sprung and Mary's end inevitable, he panicked and ran. He was afraid of what Mary's supporters would do when they found out that his duplicity had led to the end of their hopes for the restoration of the Catholic faith in England. He managed to give Christopher the slip and fled to France, without Mr. Secretary Walsingham's knowledge, approval or permission.

Sir Francis Walsingham was annoyed but not surprised by the news. "Let him go," he told Christopher. "He has served his purpose. We have the proof we need. I have no doubt his life is in enough peril without us adding to his worries. He won't be any more welcomed in France than he is here, once they discover that he tricked the French court and deceived his own Church. No, I say, let him go. The French are welcome to do what they will with him. We will now do what we must to ensure the safety of the English crown."

Anthony Babington and his co-conspirators were arrested, tried and executed on 20 September 1586. Mary, queen of Scots, was tried, found guilty and beheaded on 8 February 1587. The Catholic threat to the crown was over. Christopher Marlowe's first assignment in Her Majesty's service was a resounding success. He had played an instrumental role in saving the life of the queen and securing the Protestant faith in England.

The Letter
29 June 1587

Whereas it was reported that Christopher Morley was determined to have gone beyond the seas to Rheims and there to remain, their Lordships thought good to certify that he had no such intent, but that in all his actions he had behaved himself orderly and discretely, whereby he had done her Majesty good service and deserved to be rewarded for his faithful dealing; their Lordships' request was that the rumor thereof should be allayed by all possible means, and that he should be furthered in the degree he was to take this next Commencement, because it was not her Majesty's pleasure that any one employed, as he had been, in matters touching the benefit of his country should be defamed by those that are ignorant in the affaires he went about.

Lord Archbishop   *Lord Chancellor*   *Lord Treasurer*
Lord Chamberlaine   *Mr. Comptroler*

- Letter to Headmaster Norgate from Privy Council[i]

Christopher continued to travel to France, to watch for fallout from Mary's execution. The French were angry, but not as angry as the Spanish, who, it was reported, were planning an invasion to avenge the Catholic queen's death and gain control of this small, backwards Protestant country that was causing so many problems for the mighty Catholic empires. Christopher, in fact, spent so much time in France that, as the time of his graduation grew near and he was to receive his expected master's degree, he heard some disturbing news. The college was withholding his degree because of his prolonged absences.

Christopher wasted no time. He stormed into Headmaster Norgate's chambers. "Headmaster, you do me great offense. Why is my degree being withheld? I have met all the requirements. I have passed all the courses and exams. Why will you not grant me my degree?"

Master Norgate remained calm in the face of this attack he had been anticipating. "Marlowe, I have it on good authority that you have deceived this fine institution, this venerate college that has granted you the opportunity to pursue your studies and make something of yourself. You have accepted our charity under false pretenses. I have discovered that you are, in fact, a Catholic spy and have been going to Rheims during your absences from Corpus and training to become a Catholic priest."

Christopher exploded. "Who has accused me of such things? Name the man! Show me the evidence! No one can prove these accusations are true – I deny them all! I have been in the service of Her Majesty the Queen, and I can prove it." He slammed his fist on Norgate's desk. "By God, I can't wait to be rid of this place! I am done with the small-minded masters and timid students of this sanctuary, who run no risks and know nothing of the outside world. You have no idea what is happening outside these walls, and you don't want to know. You want to stay in your snug world, and the rest be damned. Well, you can have it."

Norgate shouted back, "Blasphemer! You take the name of the Lord in vain, you defy His will, you curse the hand that feeds you! You will live to regret your actions, mark my words. I have made my decision and that is final – no degree! Now leave my chamber at once."

Christopher's eyes narrowed. He grew calm, and said quietly, "We'll see about that," and left the room. Norgate was foolish enough to believe that he had won.

Within days, Norgate received a letter that shocked him to his core. It was signed by none other than Lord Archbishop Whitgift, Lord Treasurer Burghley, and three other members of the Privy Council. These men represented Queen Elizabeth herself in matters of great import. Their will was her will. The letter stated that Queen Elizabeth desired Christopher Marlowe, having done her Majesty great personal service, be granted his master's degree without further delay. Norgate called in his assistant. "Have the masters prepare Marlowe's degree at once."[3]

Christopher Marlowe received his master of arts degree from Cambridge University in early July 1587. The next day he entered Master Norgate's office and informed the master that he would not, in fact, be entering the holy orders, but would be leaving for London immediately to continue his service to Her Majesty the Queen of England. He presented the master with the portrait that had been hanging in Thomas Walsingham's rooms in London. Christopher said, "I know you think little of me now, Master Norgate, but mark my words, this college will be proud

---

[3] The Privy Council's letter on behalf of Christopher Marlowe is equivalent to the presidential cabinet of the United States of America interceding on behalf of a Harvard graduate student, ordering the Harvard University president to grant the student his master's degree because that student had performed a great service to the President of the United States.

to call me one of its own someday. You will see." He grinned and left the room.

Norgate would like to have burned the portrait, but given Christopher's favor with the Privy Council, he didn't dare. He took the portrait and put it in the back of his deepest closet, hoping to be rid of Christopher as quickly as possible. He didn't have long to wait – Master Norgate died four months later.

Part III
LONDON
1587-1593

The Ascent
July 1587

We'll lead you to the stately tent of war,
Where you shall hear the Scythian Tamburlaine
Threatening the world with high astounding terms,
And scourging kingdoms with his conquering sword.
View but his picture in this tragic glass,
And then applaud his fortunes as you please.

- Christopher Marlowe, *Tamburlaine the Great*

Christopher arrived in London with a new play *Tamburlaine the Great* - the title character a lowborn shepherd who uses his intellect, personality and ambition to embark on the conquest of the world. He is both vicious to his enemies and loving to his wife.

Although the title character was based on Timur "the lame," a fourteenth century Asiatic conqueror, Christopher incorporated many traits from a living person – Sir Walter Ralegh. Ralegh had made quite an impression on Christopher when he had visited Cambridge a few years earlier on a matter of business. The man who had come from low beginnings had risen to become the queen's favorite. Ralegh was rich and powerful, a study in contrasts. He had risen to glory in the early 1580s, with his brutal yet successful conquest of Ireland, during which he ordered the massacre of the captives, including women and children. Ralegh also wrote beautiful love poetry.

Again, Christopher used blank verse for *Tamburlaine*. The play had it all – vivid language, action, complexity, beautiful imagery, and strong characters consumed by overwhelming passions. He used foreign names, wove in exhibitions of wealth and stage pageantry. The play was an emblem of national pride, timely with the threat of a Spanish invasion looming over England.

Finished manuscript beneath his arm, Christopher presented his play to Philip Henslowe of the Rose Theatre, where the Admiral's Men performed. The lead part was given to a young actor by the name of Edward Alleyn, who happened to be Philip Henslowe's son-in-law. The play was performed in the fall of 1587 and became an overnight success. It set the standard for English drama, and contemporary playwrights sought to emulate Christopher's style, with varying success. The play established Christopher Marlowe's reputation as the most talented, innovative and provocative playwright of the day. So successful was *Tamburlaine* that Christopher wrote a sequel, *Tamburlaine Part II*, which proved to be just as successful. The play not only established Christopher's success as a playwright, but Edward Alleyn's reputation as the foremost actor of the day. It was the beginning of a fruitful relationship. Christopher Marlowe, the Admiral's Men and the Rose Theatre became so closely linked that the relationship would prove dangerous in the future.

***

Between 1587 and 1594, William Shakespeare disappeared. He left Stratford and his wife and children, perhaps to become a schoolmaster, or a soldier, or a lawyer – nobody knows. No records exist. He reappeared seven years later in London, listed as part owner of a newly formed theatre company, the Lord Chamberlain's Men.

The Circle

I count religion but a childish toy,
And hold there is no sin but ignorance.

- Christopher Marlowe, *Jew of Malta*

Soon after *Tamburlaine* opened at the Rose, Christopher's friend and fellow spy Thomas Walsingham invited him to a meeting, a secret meeting held late in the evening at the home of none other than Sir Walter Raleigh.

As Christopher and Thomas traveled to Sir Walter's house, Thomas told Christopher of the nature of the meeting and whom they would meet. "You know of Ralegh and his interest in the sciences. You also know that Archbishop Whitgift is highly suspicious of anyone who questions the teachings of the Church. Unfortunately, the more one knows about the sciences, and the natural order of the world, the more one questions religion. Therefore, we must meet quietly so that we are not interrupted, or worse, arrested. Far too many men who have questioned the Church have died for their beliefs. We hope to live to discover a few more truths."

Christopher's interest was certainly piqued. His days at Cambridge studying to become a clergyman had resulted in more questions than answers. "So who are these seekers of truth who are willing to risk their lives to defy Whitgift?"

"Some of the most brilliant minds in England, a true mixture of scientists and philosophers, noblemen and commoners, all interested in science and knowledge. Henry Percy, earl of Northumberland, the

"Wizard Earl" as we call him, has been a great patron of the sciences. His library is enormous and contains more books than you can imagine, on topics from astronomy to philosophy, including many that would not pass Whitgift's list of acceptable reading material. In fact, many of Northumberland's books have been banned as seditious. I find them quite illuminating. Henry Brooke, Lord Cobham is another nobleman, although personally I question his intelligence and his motives. There is something about him I don't trust, but perhaps that is because of the nature of my profession. Also, Ferdinando Stanley, Lord Strange, joins us quite often. He is a Catholic, but a reluctant one. He would rather spend his time discussing science and philosophy than religion."

Christopher was impressed. He knew that these noblemen risked not only their fortunes but their lives in their quest for knowledge, their support of the "heretical" scientists and their questioning of orthodox religious teachings.

Thomas continued, "Northumberland has supported many of the scientists you will meet tonight. Robert Hues has been around the world with Thomas Cavendish and is the tutor of Northumberland's son. He has drawn some incredible maps that have been extremely useful in understanding our physical world. I understand that his work is being used by Molyneux to create a set of globes. Another of Ralegh's seekers is Walter Warner, a mathematician, philosopher and alchemist (you know how the Church hates alchemists – likens them to witches). And the most brilliant of all, Thomas Hariot, a mathematician and astronomer who sailed with Captain John White on Ralegh's 1585 expedition to the New World. He is working on an account of the voyage - "New Found Land of Virginia" I believe is the working title. There are also many of your fellow poets and playwrights – George Chapman, Michael Drayton, Thomas Watson, Edmund Spenser, among others. It is quite a remarkable group."

When the men arrived at Durham House, they were led upstairs and entered a room full of books and men. Ralegh himself came over to greet them.

"Thomas, welcome. I'm glad you have come, and that you have brought your talented friend."

"Sir Walter, allow me to introduce Christopher Marlowe, playwright extraordinaire."

Christopher bowed. "Captain Ralegh, thank you for inviting me. I am honored to be among such men."

"Marlowe, let me say how much I enjoyed your play. You have a powerful gift. We are happy that you have joined our group. But a word of caution. The Church does not like what we do here. We keep quiet, so as not to endanger ourselves or each other. England is not yet ready for such illumination. Italy is further along, but still imprisons such men as Bruno for his beliefs about the universe."

Christopher had heard of Giordano Bruno, the Italian philosopher who had traveled to London in 1583 and become associated with Sir Philip Sidney, that great nobleman, poet, and philosopher who had died a hero's death just that past February at the battle of Zutphen. Bruno was an outspoken heretic. He defied the teachings of the Catholic Church, and was therefore welcomed in England. However, his philosophies questioned many of the Protestant teachings as well, such as the Trinity of Father, Son and Holy Ghost. Bruno's most outrageous declaration was that only God was the divine Unity. The belief was a capital offense, punishable by death. The Arian doctrine, or Unitarianism, was much discussed, albeit quietly, within the Circle.

The central tenets of the Arian doctrine were set out in the fourth century by Alexandrian Arius, who believed that Jesus was an ordinary man. In 1549, a priest by the name of John Assheton was forced by the archbishop of Canterbury to state his position on Arianism, in writing. In rebuttal, a John Proctour wrote *The Fall of the Late Arian*, quoting portions of the heresy in order to make clear his opposing arguments. A copy of this book was in Ralegh's study. Christopher wrote down large portions of the treatise. He was familiar with the argument of Unitarianism, having been exposed to the idea at Corpus Christi so that the masters had ample opportunity to label it "heresy." Christopher was not so sure. He relished the opportunity to discuss the idea with the most learned minds in England, minds that asked questions, not to dismiss the existence of God, but to understand the Truth. The men of the Circle were for the most part deeply religious, but not necessarily followers of the established Church of England, which had been in turmoil for the past half century. Because of this turmoil, the Church and the queen were intolerant of dissenters. To question the Church was to question God, and worse, the Queen. Questioning the established Church was becoming increasingly risky, and more often than not meant death.

Sir Walter spoke, "Well, gentlemen, shall we begin? I believe Hariot has some new theories for us to discuss." As the men settled into chairs, Christopher looked around the room with a smile. He had found his people at last. They called themselves Freethinkers.

The Machiavelli
1589

No, Jew; we take particularly thine
To save the ruin of a multitude,
And better one want for a common good
Than many perish for a private man.

- Christopher Marlowe, *Jew of Malta*

Christopher joined another group, in another setting. These men met in the local taverns near the Rose Theatre in Bankside. They were of a lower order – playwrights, actors, spies, hangers-on. They discussed their plays, the court, politics and religion. Christopher had much to say. His favorite topic - Niccolo Machiavelli.

Machiavelli, an Italian statesman, wrote *Il Principe*, or *The Prince*, in the early sixteenth century. The work was revolutionary. Among other principles, Machiavelli wrote that princes needed to rule by force, for the good of the masses, who were weak and evil by nature. He also wrote that many people in the Bible, specifically Moses, followed this method, sometimes killing members of his flock for the good of the group and to enforce his will. Naturally, these views were controversial, not only in Italy, where *The Prince* was banned for a number of years, but also in England, where it was banned but nevertheless widely read in the universities. Christopher had absorbed it all at Cambridge, under the noses of his esteemed masters. He felt that what Machiavelli had to say was much more truthful and realistic than what the Bible taught, and he did not hold back on sharing his views.

Today Christopher was drinking with fellow playwrights Robert Greene and Thomas Kyd.

"But Robert, you must admit, to be feared is more effective for a ruler than to be loved. Love only goes so far when the people are hungry, or when a country is at war. Then a prince must exercise force against his own people in order to maintain control. I tell you, the masses are like sheep – stupid and simple. It is for their own good. Surely you can see that. Just look around this room."

His companions stirred uneasily. They kept their eyes on their tankards. Robert Greene took a deep pull and wiped his mouth with his sleeve. Thomas Kyd looked at Christopher nervously. "Keep your voice down, Kit. Do you want to kill us all?"

Thomas Walsingham gave a light laugh. He often accompanied his friend to these haunts, after a day at the theatre. "Come, now, Thomas, surely you don't believe our words will be repeated in the Privy Council?" He, of course, knew very well what information the Privy Council has access to, and had cautioned Christopher about sharing his heretical views too loudly in public. Christopher never took notice.

"I tell you, Machiavelli had it right, no matter what princes and popes say. The Bible teaches humility, and to turn the other cheek. But where would our country be if her Majesty allowed the Catholics to run the country? Why, we would be under France or Spain by now. No, she is right. The people love her, but also fear her. Look what she did to her own cousin." Mary Stuart's execution remained fresh in the people's minds, as did the resulting attack by Spain. There was no doubt in anyone's mind that Elizabeth was not to be taken lightly, even though she was a woman. She would never blink, let alone turn the other cheek. "My friends, like it or no, there is a big difference between what the Bible teaches and what our princes do, and Niccolo Machiavelli was the first one to speak the truth."

Robert Greene turned a bleary eye on Christopher. "You will be called a heretic too if you are not careful. There are spies everywhere."

Christopher laughed. "Robert, if you had friends in high places, you would worry less. Besides, who would want to deprive the theatre of its best playwright? Come now, I will buy you another beer."

In a dark corner, two other men sat, apparently in deep conversation but listening skillfully between words. Richard Baines and Richard Cholmeley, unreliable, unintelligent, always ready to supply information (accurate or not) to the highest bidder, absorbed Christopher's every word. Cholmeley agreed with much of what Christopher had to say. Having been born into a somewhat affluent family, but coming to nothing, he was at best a supplier of intelligence and at worse an embarrassment to his employer Robert Cecil, son of William Cecil, Lord Burghley. Baines on the other hand knew that this information could be sold for a price. He had an idea of who would be willing to buy it.

The Commission
1590

Die single and thine image dies with thee.

- William Shakespeare, Sonnet 3

In the early summer of 1590, Christopher received a summons from William Cecil, Lord Burghley, her Majesty's secretary of state.

Burghley began without preamble, as was his custom. "As you know, my young ward Lord Southampton is to marry my granddaughter Lady Elizabeth de Vere, a very suitable match that I myself arranged. The problem is that the young scoundrel will have none of it. The arrangement was made a year ago, and the young man refuses to agree to the marriage. Therefore, I need your help convincing him that he must accept the arrangement and marry Lady de Vere. Your poems circulating around Gray's Inn are quite lovely, and moving. I believe that if you were to write a collection of poems encouraging him to marry, the young lord would change his mind."

Christopher laughed inwardly. Although he was flattered by Burghley's confidence in the might of his line, he doubted whether a few poems would change the young man's heart. However, he did not voice his doubts out loud. "Lord Burghley, you do me great honor. I will do everything in my power to bring this marriage to fruition. What did you have in mind?"

"Seventeen poems, one for every year of Lord Southampton's life, to be presented to him on 6 October, the day of his seventeenth birthday. I will have the sonnets bound as a birthday gift. I feel confident that these poems, commissioned especially for him, written by England's most successful poet of our day, will convince him to marry."

Christopher remained skeptical but agreed to write the sonnets, which were duly presented to Lord Southampton on his seventeenth birthday. Christopher's doubts proved right – not only did Southampton refuse to marry but he paid a penalty of five thousand pounds for the refusal. Christopher, however, not only kept his payment for the sonnets, but gained additional favor with Lord Burghley.

***

Earlier that spring, on 6 April 1590, Mr. Secretary Walsingham died. Francis Walsingham had been ambassador to France and witnessed the Bartholomew Day Massacre in August of 1572; participated in marriage negotiations between Queen Elizabeth and the French king's brother Francois, duc d'Anjou; was knighted and served as secretary of state; helped defeat the Spanish Armada; and as Elizabeth's "spymaster," broke up numerous plots against the queen's life. After a lifetime of service to Her Majesty, Francis Walsingham died heavily in debt, having financed much of England's spy network out of his own pocket. He was replaced as Secretary of State by Robert Cecil, Lord Burghley's son, an extremely intelligent and ambitious man.

Another significant event had occurred in November of the previous year – Thomas Walsingham became Lord Scadbury upon the death of his brother Edmund. He inherited title, manor and money, but not before spending a short term in debtor's prison. As Lord Scadbury, Thomas did two things – he gave up his government intelligence work and he officially became Christopher Marlowe's patron.

The tides of power were always shifting in London. Allies became enemies, stars rose and fell. In 1590 Christopher Marlowe was well placed to enjoy a long, successful career in the theatre. The audiences loved his plays, as did the queen of England, he had a wealthy patron, and he did important work for the government that gave him strong allies at court – Christopher Marlowe had it all.

The Lowlands
January 1592

The scholer sais himself to be very wel known both to the Earle of Northumberland and my lord Strang. Bains and he do also accuse one another of intent to goe to the Ennemy or to Rome.

- Letter to William Cecil, Lord Burghley
from Robert Sydney, Governor of the Low Lands[ii]

Burghley looked over the top of the letter at Christopher, seated in his office. "So, Baines got the better of you. Really, Marlowe, how careless. To be caught and accused by such a base man. His record is appalling – his word laughable. To risk exposure by such a man. Why, he's quite mad! How do you explain yourself?"

"Lord Burghley, I beg your pardon. It was quite by accident. I knew his reputation when agreeing to share rooms with him and the goldsmith Gilbert, but as you know he was not the target of my mission to the Lowlands. I never meant to become involved in his affairs. But one day I came into our chambers and there he was with Gilbert, holding a pewter coin they had just struck. Baines started screaming that I had been the one to strike the coin. Immediately the room contained several officials, who must have been lingering nearby, perhaps on call, and they arrested me. My only recourse was to accuse Baines of the same, to throw confusion on the proceedings."

"But to implicate Northumberland and Strange? Why, man, you have practically put their heads on the block. To be associated with a common coiner, never mind a lowly informer!"

63

"My lord, I would be in prison yet. I had to gain my freedom. I didn't mention Captain Ralegh. Besides, Sir Robert will not talk. He owes you and the queen much. The lords will not encounter any trouble over this."

"Still in all, I would that you had never become involved with Baines. That man is trouble. He creates trouble wherever he treads. Mind you stay clear of him from now on. I can not afford to lose you as an agent. The queen needs you, and so do I."

"Your Lordship, you do me great honor. You have my word, Richard Baines will never get in my way again. He is an insignificant toad whom I can best in any situation. He was simply angry that I referred to an incident in Rheims back in 1582 – he tried to poison the seminary well. I ridiculed him in my new play *Jew of Malta*. He had quite a time getting out of our predicament, much harder than I did. He will not soon forget the lesson to be learned when crossing Christopher Marlowe."

The Descent
August 1592

Wonder not (for with thee will I first begin), thou famous gracer of tragedians, that Greene, who hath said with thee, like the fool in his heart, There is no God.... Is it pestilent Machiavellian policy that thou hast studied.

Yes, trust them not: for there is an upstart crow, beautified with our feathers, that with his tiger's heart wrapt in a player's hide, supposes he is as well able to bombast out a blank-verse as the best of you: and being an absolute Johannes factotum, is in his own conceit the only Shake-scene in a country.

- Robert Greene, *Groats-worth of Wit.*[iii]

Henry Chettle was worried. "But Robert, I can't print this! You will condemn your friends to death. To accuse Christopher Marlowe of atheism, in print no less. Are you mad? Why would you do such a thing?"

Robert Greene picked feverishly at his bed covers. He knew he would not leave his bed again. "I tell you, it must be said! That man will end up like me, dying penniless and alone. He must stop his wicked ways, before it is too late. He says there is no God! Can you imagine? He says after all his years studying to be a clergyman, he believes we are in control of our own destinies, not God. He will burn in hell, I say! I must stop him before it is too late. Even if it is too late for him, maybe I can save my own soul."

"Robert, please reconsider. Marlowe is Lord Burghley's man. In fact, he has many powerful friends. I tell you, I won't do it!"

Greene lifted himself from the bed with a frail arm. "Playwriting has been the ruin of me. Please, Henry, I beg you. Please print my work, as my final request."

"But what of Edward Alleyn? Why bring him into this? He is the most famous actor in the theatre. So what if he has written a play? To call him an "upstart crow," a Shake-scene who bellows his lines on the stage, a *Johannes factotum* jack-of-all-trades. He and his father-in-law Henslowe will bring ruin upon me. I can't afford to offend them."

"Alleyn *is* a jack-of-all-trades. To think a mere actor can write a play. He needs to stick with acting. Marlowe had it right – Alleyn has a tiger's heart wrapped in a player's hide."

Chettle protested. "Marlowe was referring to a woman, Margaret, in one of his *Henry VI* plays. The line by York is "tiger's hart wrapped in a *woman's* hide.""

"I know perfectly well what the line is! You think I don't know every line that wretched Marlowe has written? I was writing plays while he was still in school. And then in he comes with the likes of *Tamburlaine* and *The Jew*. To think an atheist should have such success! He will not go unpunished! Please, Henry, please publish *Groatsworth*. My soul, Marlowe's and possibly yours depend on it."

Chettle finally relinquished. "All right, my friend, I will grant you this final request, although I don't doubt I shall live to regret it."

"Thank you, my friend. You'll see – Marlowe will thank you as well, in the end."

Robert Greene died 3 September 1592. It is not known whether his soul was saved or not, but he significantly damaged Christopher Marlowe's reputation and alerted the Privy Council to Christopher's atheistic views.

The Libel
5 May 1593

Weele cutte your throtes, in your temples praying
Not paris massacre so much blood did spill.
[signed]Tamberlaine

- The Dutch Church Libel[iv]

Richard Cholmeley was a dangerous man. He fancied himself an intellectual, being from a family of landed gentry. His brother Sir Hugh served the local government of Cheshire. Richard posed as a Catholic to entrap priests, whom he duly turned over to the Protestant authorities, for a price.

Cholmeley arranged a meeting with Christopher Marlowe, under the guise of having valuable information to pass along. As they sat in the corner of a dark tavern, Cholmeley listened to Marlowe and liked what he heard. Never one to hold back, Marlowe told Cholmeley of his religious views and of the Circle, which he said was fighting ignorance in the Church. Marlowe even mentioned their leader, Sir Walter Ralegh, who was on record as opposing the queen's protection of foreign merchants who were taking trade away from Londoners. Cholmeley was very impressed with Marlowe's connection to Ralegh, and Marlowe's skill in writing plays. Cholmeley was also mentally unbalanced. He asked to be admitted into the Circle but was refused. Then he became angry.

He decided to write a treatise on the foreigners who were ruining the city, namely the Dutch Protestant merchants who had fled religious persecution in their country. Queen Elizabeth had promised protection to anyone who chose to defy the pope. To oppose the Protestant refugees in England was to oppose the Queen herself. Dangerous business. Cholmeley liked it that way.

He wrote his diatribe in iambic pentameter, Marlowe's chosen style, and he included several references from Marlowe's plays. He even signed it "Tamburlaine." He accused the authorities of profiting from the Dutch merchants – that was sure to get their attention. He decided to show the treatise to someone he knew was no supporter of Marlowe, the Circle or especially Ralegh – Archbishop Whitgift.

Cholmeley knew he would never be granted access to the archbishop himself, so he sent a message to Whitgift's secretary Benedict, stating that he had important information for the safety of the crown, and that the information would also serve as evidence against the archbishop's adversary Walter Ralegh. Ralegh had long been a favorite of the queen, but Whitgift meant to change that.

Cholmeley was granted an audience with Benedict. He showed him the treatise, the libel against the foreign merchants that he intended to post on the door of the Dutch Church. Benedict knew his master would be pleased. The treatise implied that Ralegh's follower Christopher Marlowe was anti-foreigner and thus anti-crown. It also accused government officials of being corrupt, but not Church officials. Benedict paid Cholmeley a small sum and assured him of his master's pleasure.

Cholmeley left well pleased. Early on the morning of 5 May, he posted his treatise on the door of the Dutch Church, where it was soon found and reported to the Privy Council. They were not amused.

The Star Chamber
11 May 1593

Aucthorize you to make search and aprehend everie person so to be suspected, and for that purpoze to enter into al houses and places where anie such maie be remayning, and upon their aprehencion to make like search in anie the chambers, studies, chestes or other like places for al manner of writings or papers that may geve you light for the discoverie of the libellers.... you shal by aucthoritie hereof put them to the torture in Bridewel.

Lord Archbishop   *Earl of Derby.*

Lord Keeper   *Lord Buckhurst.*

Lord Treasurer   *Sir Robert Cecill*

Sir John Fortescue.

- Letter issued from Star Chamber[v]

Archbishop Whitgift slammed his hand on the table. "It's treason, I say! Her Majesty's law is being questioned, and that means treason. The libels have become more blatant with each passing day, and this is the worst. I will know who wrote this, and he will be punished."

"Lord Archbishop, I think I may know who wrote this libel." Sir John Puckering, Lord Keeper, spoke for the first time during the meeting. "My sources tell me that the libel could have been written by none other than Christopher Marlowe, the playwright. His *Jew of Malta*, which is very popular in the playhouse, speaks of Machiavelli, which was referred to in the libel. Also, it was signed Tamburlaine, another of Marlowe's characters."

"Lord Archbishop." William Cecil, Lord Treasurer Burghley, broke in. "Really, why would Marlowe write such a piece and all but sign his name to it? Surely someone else wrote it, to implicate him in this treasonous matter."

"Nevertheless, we must question the man. I do not doubt it was he. To go through university and fail to take holy orders, to walk away from all that was given to him, to walk away from God and Church, to become nothing but a playwright. Six years ago we sat in this very room and ordered his college to grant him his degree. I am still suspicious of his absences during college, but you and Sir Robert here persuaded me of his innocence, saying he had served the queen in some capacity. But I am still in the dark. I do not believe what I was told, and I mean to find the truth."

"Lord Archbishop, there is more." Sir John's eyes glinted with anticipation. "I am also told that Marlowe is included within Walter Ralegh's heretical circle. These men gather in private rooms and speak blasphemy, questioning the Bible, our lord Jesus and even the Creator himself. I tell you, the queen is not safe from men who question such things. It is treason, I tell you, against queen and country."

Father and son looked at each other, powerless to stop the flow of anger and righteous indignation in the room. They felt a chill for the man they had both come to respect and rely upon. Now they must do what they could to warn him of his danger and to protect him from the vengeful and powerful archbishop.

The archbishop continued. "Lord Keeper, bring Christopher Marlowe in. I am interested in what he has to say about his circle of fellow atheists."

Sir John licked his lips. "I am afraid that is not possible at the moment. You see, he is out of the city, living at Scadbury Manor in Chislehurst with his patron Sir Thomas Walsingham. I assume he went to avoid the plague, as I wish I could were we not needed here to serve the queen."

"Sir Thomas, eh? Well, it seems our man Marlowe has many influential friends." Whitgift glanced briefly at the Cecils. "Never mind, we will begin by getting to know his lower circle. Have his fellow playmakers come in. I would hear what they know about this atheist circle. If we can catch a few of them as well, so much the better."

Again Puckering spoke. "I know with whom to start. Thomas Kyd is a playmaker and friend of Marlowe. He is said to be writing a play about Thomas More, that traitor who died for his sins against good King Henry. We will see how he fares on the rack."

By now Burghley and his son were thoroughly alarmed. One of their most valuable agents was in danger of being tortured and revealing secrets the Cecils relied upon to maintain their hold on power within Elizabeth's court. Yes, the Cecils were very alarmed indeed.

The Betrayal
12 May 1593

Vile hereticall Conceiptes Denyinge the Deity of Jesus Christ our Saviour fownd amongst the papers of Thos Kydd prisoner Which he affirmeth that he had ffrom Marlowe.

-Thomas Kyd's statement from Bridwell Prison.[vi]

Thomas Kyd screamed in pain. His body had been stretched to the breaking point on the rack. Richard Topcliffe waited patiently. The queen's rack master was practiced in his profession and took it seriously, to keep Her Majesty and realm safe. His job was to expose threats to the crown, and he excelled in obtaining confessions, true or not.

"You are a traitor to the crown. Your play *Thomas More* is seditious and shows you wish for the queen's fall from the throne. Do you wish for the playgoers to riot and overthrow the queen? Who is working with you? Who helped you write the play? We know there were other hands, since one of them led to you, but we want the others as well. Speak quickly, before I take another turn."

"I tell you, we meant no offense. We only wished to write a play of the times, which speaks to the city's unease of foreigners. In this time of plague, we must attract an audience. The theatres will open any day, I am sure. The owners are desperate for a new play, and I needed the money. Sir, I beg of you, I meant no offense."

Topcliffe looked impassively at the figure on the rack. "There is also the matter of the treatise."

Kyd looked up. "The treatise? What treatise?"

Topcliffe nodded to his assistant, who turned the arm of the rack.

When the screams subsided, Topcliffe asked the question again. "The treatise - how did it get in your room? Who does it belong to?"

The treatise in question was John Proctour's *Fall of the Late Arian*. In his counter-response to John Assheton's argument that Christ was not equal to God, Proctour had quoted large segments of the original Unitarian declaration, as heretical in 1593 as when Assheton had first penned it more than forty years before.

The man on the rack gasped out, "I have told you, I do not know. It does not belong to me. I love God and my queen." Tears streamed down Kyd's face, and he made his decision. "The treatise must belong to Marlowe, Christopher Marlowe, with whom I shared rooms two years since. His papers must somehow have been mixed with mine and he left without them. I tell you, I am innocent. Marlowe is the man you want."

Topcliffe smiled with satisfaction. He knew Sir John Puckering and Archbishop Whitgift would be pleased. They had asked for information that would implicate Christopher Marlowe, and now Topcliffe could provide it. The charges against Marlowe had just gone from libel to heresy. The fact that heretical language was found among papers belonging to Marlowe, even though the treatise ultimately supported the conventional religious beliefs of the time, was enough to call for Marlowe's arrest. Topcliffe's assistant carefully transcribed the statement, knowing that the document would be used as an indictment. Topcliffe was nothing if not thorough at his job.

The torture master looked at the broken body before him. "Very well. You have named another to save yourself. Whether it is the truth or not, we shall see. You will be kept here until the Star Chamber questions Marlowe and orders your release." He turned to leave, then turned back. "Some refuse to name another, and go to their deaths with a clear conscience. Others, such as yourself, would rather live with guilt than die with virtue. May God have mercy on your soul." He left to the sound of sobbing.

The Arrest
18 May 1593

Warrant to Henry Maunder one of the Messengers of her Ma[jesty's] Chamber to repair to the house of Mr Tho: Walsingham in Kent, or to anie other place where he shall understand Christofer Marlow to be remaining, and by vertue hereof to apprehend and bring him to the Court in his Companie. And in case of need to require ayd.

-Warrant for Christopher Marlowe's arrest.[vii]

Christopher looked up from his writing desk. He had been working on a poem, a sister to his *Venus and Adonis*, which was a good poem but one that lacked mastery and depth. Christopher had come to Scadbury Manor to rework the poem. In fact, he was rewriting it. The peace and fresh air at Chislehurst helped clear his head. Lately he was having trouble working.

He heard a horse approaching at a fast pace. Christopher put his quill aside and stood up. For some reason his heart beat faster.

The horse crossed the drawbridge and pulled up in the yard. The rider handed the reins to the stable boy and strode to the house. Christopher heard the servant open the door and the rider begin to speak. He started down the stairs.

The rider introduced himself as Henry Maunder, messenger of Her Majesty's Chamber. Christopher watched from the stairs as the rider was shown into Thomas Walsingham's study. His heart beat even faster as he walked down the stairs and listened to the two men talking.

"Your lordship, please pardon the intrusion. I come by order of Her Majesty with a warrant for Christopher Marlowe's arrest. I understand he is here living at Scadbury Manor."

"On what grounds? He has done no offense. Christopher Marlowe has been living here under my patronage for the past three weeks."

"My lord, that is for the Privy Council to decide. They have evidence that Marlowe is an atheist and would have him answer the charges. I am to bring him to the Chamber at once."

Thomas was silent a moment. His hands gripped the desk in fear. "Wait here. I will find him." He walked to the door of his chamber and saw Christopher standing on the stairs. "You heard?"

"Yes, I heard." Christopher gave a light laugh. "So Whitgift has fabricated some sordid little story about me? I knew it was only a matter of time. I knew when I turned my back on the Church that he would come after me. I do not doubt that his true targets are Sir Walter and the others of the Circle. I wonder who pointed the finger to me? I will learn soon enough, I suppose."

Thomas walked over to his friend and put a hand on his shoulder. "My friend, make no mistake, you are in danger. Whitgift is no fool. He is cunning and powerful. If he sees an opportunity to become more powerful, he will take it. He has had his eye on the Circle for some time now and means to destroy it. You, my friend, are a small but significant means to Whitgift's end purpose. I will do what I can for you, but I'm afraid Whitgift is in control now. He has overpowered even Lord Burghley himself, something I never would have believed. I can only imagine what

Lord Burghley and Sir Robert have to say about all of this. I do not doubt they tried to stop it but were powerless. No, my friend, this does not bode well."

Christopher gave another laugh. "Come now, Thomas, do not be so glum. You underestimate our allies. The Cecils will not let me fall – I am too valuable. Have I not proven myself in service to the queen? The queen herself knows this. And does she not love my plays? Why, she would never let her favorite playwright go down."

Thomas gripped Christopher by both shoulders and shook him. "Why, man, don't be a fool. You know how powerful Whitgift has become. You know he has many supporters. The people are uneasy. The crops have failed, the plague is upon us again, the masses from the continent are squeezing Londoners so they can hardly draw breath, let alone feed their families. Whitgift will seize any opportunity to lay the blame on his enemies. And right now, anyone who asks too many questions, especially about the Church, is his enemy. I tell you, the Circle is in danger, and you are a link. Do not take this lightly."

Christopher looked at his friend with steady eyes. "Yes, I know this is serious. I know that I am a mere player in this game of life and death. The Circle was formed because of small-minded men like Whitgift. I will not let it be destroyed because of me, I give you my word."

"What are you going to do?"

"I will go with Maunder and appear before the Chamber. I have no doubt that Lord Burghley will do what he can for me. He still has some influence. I will hope for the best."

"May God go with you, my friend. I will do what I can to learn of the charges and help with your defense. I have someone in London who will keep me apprised of the proceedings."

"Thank you, Thomas. You have been more than a patron to me these past few years. I value your friendship above all others. Somehow we will prevail."

Thomas did not reply. He doubted very much a happy end to this terrible story. But he only said, "Go pack your things. I will arrange for a horse." With a heavy heart he watched his friend walk up the stairs. He knew Christopher's days of freedom were over.

The Window
20 May 1593

This day Christofer Marley of London, gent. Being sent for by warrant from their Lordships hath entered his apparance accordinglie for his Indemnity herein; and is commaunded to giue his daily attendaunce on their Lordships, until he shalbe licensed to the Contrary.

- Christopher Marlowe's release on bail.[viii]

  Christopher stood before the members of the Star Chamber, whose primary function was to punish those accused of slanders, libels and riots. This court was not limited by statutes and acted at the will of the presiding member, the archbishop of Canterbury. The court had the power to, among other things, authorize torture, which it did if not openly, routinely. It operated behind closed doors, and records of the proceedings in the 1590s do not exist. Nor were the accused allowed legal counsel. It was before this powerful, autocratic group that Christopher Marlowe pleaded his innocence.

  "My Lords, I beg of you, why would I write such a libel as that posted on the Dutch Church door? To have all but signed my name to it, knowing that I must surely end up here, before this court, as I now am? And the Arian treatise, I admit it to be mine, but my Lords, the treatise is *against* the heretic Assheton. Proctour *refuted* the Unitarian doctrine. That is what the treatise states, even though it uses some heretical language of Assheton's. Proctour uses Assheton's words as examples of his illogic. I beg you to read the treatise for yourselves, to prove my words are true."

Archbishop Whitgift thundered from his chair in the middle of the judge's table. "Do not speak to me of reading that filth! This is not the first time you have turned your back on God, not the first time you have been involved in heresy, not the first time you have defied the Church. You believe yourself to be above the Church, you and your School of Atheism. You think I know nothing of what goes on with your leaders Ralegh and Northumberland? They think they are beyond my reach, that they enjoy the protection of the queen, but the queen herself will not stand for this heresy, this act against God. The queen herself gives this court the power to punish traitors like you, and that is what this court will do."

The room grew quiet as the archbishop's words trailed up through the smoky air of the Star Chamber and rose to the stars painted on the ceiling of the room in Westminster Palace, from which the chamber derived its name. Christopher was sure the members could hear his beating heart. Then Lord Treasurer Burghley began to speak.

"My Lords, surely justice must be served. If this man Marlowe, who has proved valuable to the queen in his service during the Babington Plot, is guilty of heresy, then he of course must be condemned. But it is our duty to establish his guilt, not presume it. I have found this man to be a trustworthy servant of Her Majesty, with nothing to cast doubt over his integrity" (the Baines coining episode in the Lowlands flitted briefly through both the minds of Burghley and Christopher, but was immediately dismissed). "I would read this treatise, and judge it for myself. Then may we condemn or release this man."

The other members of the court stirred. All were aware of the power struggle between Archbishop Whitgift, whose power was on the rise in this time of social unrest and religious turmoil, and Lord Burghley, whose influence with the queen was not as strong as it had once been. The archbishop was gaining the advantage, but Burghley was not done yet. The members still respected and listened to him, and more than a few were alarmed at Whitgift's power and ambition.

The earl of Derby spoke. "Lord Archbishop, I would see for myself this heretical treatise before I condemn this man Marlowe. As Lord Burghley has said, if we find the treatise to be heretical, then surely he must be condemned." Not only did the earl resent the Archbishop's overzealous attitude, his son Lord Strange was the patron of a company of players.

Now the Lord Chamberlain spoke. He, too, disliked Whitgift's powerful hold, and also enjoyed Marlowe's plays. "Lord Archbishop, I agree with Lord Derby. Let us review the treatise and see if it is indeed heretical. This Marlowe has been of good service to the queen. I would not lose him in an error of judgment."

Whitgift remained silent. He knew that Burghley still had influence over the queen, and that Burghley relied heavily on the worm before the court for secret intelligence. Whitgift also knew that a certain Richard Baines was at that very moment compiling damming evidence that would be the final nail in Marlowe's coffin. "Very well. I see that this court has accepted the pleadings of a dangerous heretic. I myself have no doubts, but since we are reasonable men, I will release Marlowe on bail. He is to present himself to this court on a daily basis. Failure to do so will prove his guilt, and he will be condemned." He turned to Christopher. "You have many powerful friends, for such a lowly playwright. They have saved you thus far, but they cannot protect you forever. I wonder that you are willing to risk their lives as well as your own. Rest assured, God will be the final judge." With that, Christopher was dismissed and returned to Chislehurst.

The Nail
27 May 1593

A note contaynineg the opinion of one Christopher Marley

He affirmeth that Moyses was but a Jugler, & that one Heriots being Sir W Raleighs man can do more then he.

That one Ric Cholmley hath Confessed that he was persuaded by Marloe's Reasons to become an Atheist.

- The Baines Note[ix]

Richard Baines's eyes glittered with hatred, and madness. He had worked hard on his report, and knew the archbishop would be pleased. The note had it all – Marlowe's blasphemies against the Church, his association with Sir Walter Ralegh, his coining in the Lowlands, and his conversion of Richard Cholmeley to atheism.

Baines knew he was repeating much of his own confession at Rheims, back in 1582 when he had been caught trying to poison the seminary's well. He had been posing as a Catholic priest, while in fact plotting to kill Dr. William Allen, the head of the Catholic college. That filthy playwright Marlowe had heard of Baines's disgrace and mocked him, in public no less, in his play *Jew of Malta*.

Baines had spent a year in a French prison, and on 13 May 1583 signed a confession for Dr. Allen describing his fall into wickedness, his wavering faith in the Catholic Church, and his attempts to convert Catholics to Protestantism, under the employment of Queen Elizabeth's spymaster Sir Francis Walsingham.

His motives, he said, were ambition and greed.

Expelled from Rheims, Baines made his way back to England. He still provided occasional intelligence to Walsingham, but a shadow now hung over him. That shadow grew much darker in 1592 after the Lowlands incident, when he had thought that by turning in that wretched Christopher Marlowe for coining, he might return himself to favor. But things had not gone according to plan. Francis Walsingham had died three years previously, and it was Marlowe who had somehow gained the favor of the Cecils. Baines found himself once again at the displeasure of those he hoped to serve. And he blamed Marlowe entirely.

Gathering evidence against Marlowe had not been difficult. The playwright frequented taverns and freely gave his opinions about religion and politics. While his plays had to remain conservative in order to pass the censor, Christopher had no hesitation about sharing his personal views with anyone who would listen. He scoffed at his friends' cautions. Truth be told, Marlowe was a powerful speaker and the less intelligent - people like Richard Cholmeley - hung on his every word. Marlowe also enjoyed the protection of very powerful men, not least Walter Ralegh and Robert Cecil. So Baines kept his mouth shut and his ears open, until he had gathered enough information for his report.

By the end of the month he was ready. On 27 May he submitted his report to Richard Bancroft, canon of Westminster and Archbishop Whitgift's private chaplain, on behalf of Her Majesty Queen Elizabeth. In return, Baines received from Archbishop

Whitgift the rectorship for Waltham in Lincolnshire, which he held until the end of his days.

The Retribution
29 May 1593

That he saieth & verely beleveth that one Marlowe is able to showe more sounde reasons for Atheisme then any devine in Englande is able to geve to prove devinitie & that Marloe tolde him that hee hath read the Atheist lecture to Sir walter Raliegh & others-

- Remembrances of wordes & matters against Ric Cholmeley[x]

Thomas Drury also spent time in the taverns. He listened to Marlowe's scandalous talk and knew it would come in useful one day. But Drury's hatred was not directed at Marlowe and was not associated with his opinions on the Church. Thomas Drury had a score to settle with Richard Cholmeley, and his employers would pay handsomely if he could discredit the Privy Council as well. Drury got to work. In his "Remembrances " he managed to indict the Council, discredit Marlowe, and thus Ralegh.

Drury sent the letter to Anthony Bacon, brother to the statesman and intellectual Francis Bacon. He knew his report would also reach the hands of Robert Devereux, the powerful earl of Essex and patron of the Bacon brothers. It was well known in the queen's court that her courtiers fought for power – Ralegh and his supporters against Essex and his supporters. For good measure the Church, represented by Archbishop Whitgift, and the government, represented by William and Robert Cecil, were thrown into the mix. Intrigue was everywhere, loyalties switched by the minute and spies turned on spies for a few pounds. A very dangerous game of life and death. The skilled ones stayed alive.

Drury was by no means one of the skilled ones. He had landed in prison because the informer Richard Cholmeley had turned him into the authorities in May of 1591, on "divers great and fond matters." Two years later it was Drury's chance for revenge. Anthony Bacon and Essex wanted to bury the Cecils and undermine the Council in general. They promised a reward. Drury delivered his indictment, and his reward was to be hauled off to prison again.

He had failed to recognize that by accusing the entire Council, except Archbishop Whitgift, of misconduct, he would be jeopardizing his freedom. Henry Carey, the Lord Chamberlain, in particular took exception to Drury's accusations and ordered his arrest. Drury appealed to Anthony Bacon from prison, begging both for his release and payment for services rendered. He was denied both.

By 17 August, Drury had had enough of the Essex faction. He appealed to Robert Cecil and was granted both his freedom and employment. From then on, Thomas Drury was Robert Cecil's man. Cecil had just as good reason for discrediting Ralegh – less power for Ralegh meant more for Robert Cecil. A simple game for Cecil to play – and he was very good at it.

Amid all the power struggles, Christopher's neck was in an ever-tightening noose. He knew he was in serious trouble and unless he came up with a plan, he would be imprisoned, tortured, and put to death as a heretic and traitor to the crown. The Freethinkers would be in jeopardy, and his friends, one by one, would meet a similar fate. Then Christopher received word at Scadbury Manor from Lord Burghley.

The Lamb
29 May 1593
St. Thomas-a-Watering

Wherein, notwithstanding the surprising of the printer, he maketh it known unto the world that he feareth neither proud priest, antichristian pope, tyrannous prelate, nor godless catercap, but defieth all the race of them by these presents, and offereth conditionally, as is farther expressed herein, by open disputation to appear in the defence of his cause against them and theirs.

- The Protestation of Martin Marprelate[xi]

John Penry was not afraid. He faced his inevitable death with a clear head and a calm heart. He did, however, regret not saying goodbye to his wife and children – there was no time. Penry's rushed execution prevented him from completing many things he had wished to do. Still, some might say he had done plenty.

While awaiting his execution, Penry wrote to Lord Burghley and the earl of Essex, protesting his loyalty to the Queen in hopes of a lesser sentence. His pleas were unanswered. John Penry went to his death knowing that he had sacrificed his life for his religious and moral beliefs, but he did not know that his body would be used to save another man's life. That man was Christopher Marlowe.

While Marlowe attended Corpus Christi College at Cambridge, John Penry attended Peterhouse, another college of Cambridge University. Both took their B.A.s. Then Penry moved on to Oxford to take his M.A. while Marlowe stayed at Cambridge to take his. While at Oxford, Penry became a Puritan preacher who denounced Archbishop Whitgift's strict repression and censorship of Puritan doctrine. In 1586 the Archbishop had been empowered by the Star Chamber to control all the printing in England, and Whitgift used his power to crush any and all attempts to weaken the nascent Anglican Church. His main target was the Puritans.

Between 1588 and 1589, Penry printed the "Marprelate Tracts," a series of seven pamphlets by anonymous writers using the pseudonym Martin Marprelate, in which Archbishop Whitgift was named, in a word, the Antichrist. Naturally, the Archbishop was furious, and the hunt for the authors was on. Penry had to move his printing press to many locations around the country to avoid discovery. He even spent some time in Scotland to avoid capture. However, in September 1592 Penry returned to England. He was arrested in March 1593 after being identified by a London vicar and brought to trial 21 May 1593. On 25 May John Penry was sentenced to death by hanging.

John Penry's death sentence was Christopher Marlowe's salvation. When Lord Burghley received Penry's plea for commutation, he knew he had found a way to save Marlowe, a valuable and loyal servant to the Queen. A good way to avoid persecution is to be dead. It was too late for John Penry, but not too late for Marlowe. Lord Burghley made contact with the men he knew could carry out his plan. He arranged a meeting at Deptford, some two miles from St. Thomas-a-Watering, where John Penry would be put to death. Burghley sent word to Thomas Walsingham at Scadbury Manor, telling Marlowe to hasten to Deptford, where plans would be put into action.

Late in the afternoon, an unusual hour for an execution, on 29 May, John Penry was put to death. There were no family or friends present. His body was not returned to his wife, nor was she allowed to view the body, which was buried in an unmarked grave. To this day, the location of his grave is unknown.

The Death
30 May 1593
Deptford

The prey of worms, my body being dead;
The coward conquest of a wretch's knife

-William Shakespeare, Sonnet 74

Ever since her husband's death three years previously, Dame Eleanor Bull, a kinswoman of Lord Burghley, had run a respectable lodging house in the small bustling port of Deptford, some twelve miles southeast of London off the river Thames. She also provided the occasional quiet place to conduct government business, official or not. Christopher Marlowe and Ingram Frizer waited impatiently in the room Dame Eleanor had prepared for them. They had much to discuss. The two other men arrived midmorning.

"My apologies." Robert Poley didn't look the least apologetic. He never did. "We were detained at the border, but I managed to talk our way through." He always did.

"Never mind. We must get to work." Christopher paced nervously. "We all know by now that Archbishop Whitgift is trying to get to Ralegh and Northumberland through me. Whitgift knows Ralegh still has many supporters, including the queen, although he is out of favor at the moment. Whitgift cannot get to Ralegh directly, especially when he is fighting Burghley as well. This is why Whitgift is using these roundabout tactics to penetrate the Circle. He wants to arrest me and see what Topcliffe can get out of me at Bridwell.

He looked at the other men in the group - Ingram Frizier, long-time servant of Thomas Walsingham, Nicholas Skeres, court messenger, secret agent, and conman, and Richard Poley, a man to be respected and feared. It was Poley, aided by Skeres, who had convinced Anthony Babington of their friendship, which proved false and had led Babington and his fellow conspirators to their deaths. Christopher knew the man to be ruthless.

Christopher continued, "Lord Burghely has devised a plan. I will not report to the Star Chamber today, nor will they find me at Scadbury Manor this time. The archbishop will waste no time beginning the hunt. We must give him a reason to stop looking. In short, we will fake my death, here in Deptford now that the queen is in residence at Greenwich Palace. Because Deptford is within twelve miles of Greenwich, we are within the Verge, which means the queen's court has jurisdiction over murders and such. Therefore, Her Majesty's coroner William Danby will preside over the inquest. The local authorities need not be involved at all. Lord Burghley has informed Her Majesty of the situation, and she is in agreement, although she does not wish anyone to know of her involvement."

"What is the plan?" The three other men were practiced conmen, especially when there was money to be made.

"Lord Burghley has sent word that the Puritan preacher John Penry was put to death last evening at St. Thomas-a-Watering, just two miles from here. Sir William has arranged for the body to be "removed" to a secure location, and we are to bring the body back here tonight and switch it for mine.

The men spent the day in deep discussion, devising a full-proof way for Christopher Marlowe to "die" and end the archbishop's persecution.

Ingram Frizer had strong reservations. "So you mean to produce a body, disfigure the face and pass it off as Marlowe? What if the jury is not fooled? I don't want to hang! What if the jury doesn't believe I'm innocent? What if they say I did it on purpose, or it was my fault?"

"Why, man, how will the jury know? The inquest will be held here in Deptford, where Marlowe is known to no one. After I get through with the body, the poor sod's own mother wouldn't recognize him." Poley smiled devilishly. "I'm telling ye, man. Skeres and I convince them. They're a bunch of country folk. I have fooled the gentry. You won't hang."

Christopher looked at Poley. "Thomas Walsingham is a generous man. I have no doubt you are being well rewarded for your services. But make no mistake, Poley. Upon my word, if you accept more money to betray us, your life will be forfeited. Now let's be off."

**

Frizer eyed the body. "Were you seen?"

Again, Poley laughed, "Aye, but no matter. These country folk are not too keen. They think the poor sod is drunk."

The three men arranged the body on the bed behind the table, as if it had fallen backward from the table onto the bed.

When Poley was satisfied with the arrangement, he said, "Skeres, go fetch the constable. We must be quick." He turned towards Frizer. "Now for you." Before Frizer could protest, Poley drew Frizer's dagger and slashed Frizer's head twice with his own knife, leaving two red trails. Frizer clutched his head. "You devil, you might have given me warning. You are practiced with violence."

Poley merely lay the knife down on the floor near the bed. "It is what we arranged. It had to be done, the quicker the better."

"Yes, but you didn't have to enjoy the deed so much," muttered Frizer. He sat on the bed beside the body holding a cloth to his head.

The constable arrived within twenty minutes. "How now, what is this? A murder? You London gentlemen have been up to mischief. I do not like such dealings in my town."

Poley began his tale. "Sir, upon my life, this man Marlowe would have killed us all. Crazy he was, over the reckoning of the bill. He said we should pay, since we invited him here, but we wanted to split the payment. Then he became violent. Frizer here was fighting for his life, I tell you. It was him or Marlowe."

The constable stuck out his chin. "That is for the jury to decide. I will make all the arrangements."

Poley coughed quietly then said, "I beg your pardon, Constable, but the queen is in residence at Greenwich, meaning that your fair town is within the Verge. Her majesty's coroner Danby has jurisdiction over criminal matters now. He will preside at the inquest."

"Yes, of course. I had but forgotten. I will send for Danby at once. You men must come with me. You will stay in our jail until the inquest. I will post a guard at this door – nothing must be disturbed."

Poley thought to himself, "Never fear, little man. The stage has been set perfectly."

The Inquest
1 June 1593

Where-upon the said Ingram, in fear of being slain, & sitting in the manner aforesaid between the said Nicholas Skeres & Robert Poley so that he could not in any wise get away, in his own defense & for the saving of his life, then & there struggled with the said Christopher Morley to get back from him his dagger aforesaid; in which affray the same Ingram could not get away from the said Christopher Morley;...& so it befell in that affray that the said Ingram, in defense of his life, with the dagger aforesaid to the value of 12d, gave the said Christopher then & there a mortal wound over his right eye of the depth of two inches & of the width of one inch; of which mortal wound the aforesaid Christopher Morley then & there instantly die.

- Coroner's Report on the Death of
Christopher Marlowe[xii]

Two days after Christopher's "death," sixteen men assembled as the jury for the inquest. They were all respectable men from Deptford and its immediate surroundings, and all had viewed the body. They did not know the dead man, nor his killer, as both were from London. Coroner William Danby arrived on the scene in a surprisingly short amount of time and refused to have the local coroner present, counter to custom.

Coroner Danby began. "Will the defendant please stand before the jury? Now, sir, you must tell the jury truthfully what happened."

Ingram Frizer began his tale. "Coroner Danby, upon my life, I never meant to kill anyone. Marlowe, Skeres, Poley and I arranged to meet here in Deptford to conclude some business. It was somewhat delicate, involving a large sum of money. Some of the money went missing, so to speak. We were interested in finishing this business, because Marlowe was in trouble with the Star Chamber no less. Word was that he was to go to London and face charges of atheism. We talked over the matter all day, at Dame Eleanor's house. She provided us dinner and supper in the upper room where you saw the body. After supper, tempers ran high, being as no one could account for where the money had gone. I believe Marlowe was thinking about the Star Chamber more than he was about the money. I was sitting at the table with Skeres and Poley on either side of me. Marlowe was lying on the bed behind us. He then accused me of taking the money, and before I knew what was happening, he drew my dagger from my belt and slashed me on the head twice. Crazy he was, yelling and swearing that he would kill me and all the other no account cozeners. I tell you, I thought I was dead for sure. But I turned and grabbed his hand and somehow managed to get my knife away from him. Before I knew what I was doing, I plunged the dagger into his eye. He fell back onto the bed, twitched a bit, and that was all. Please, Coroner Danby, I swear this is the truth. I beg you, please don't hang me. It wasn't my fault." Frizer had tears in his eyes.

Danby was concerned – Frizer was a fine actor, but the tale was weak. This is the best Lord Burghley's people could come up with? Why, the jury would see right through this ridiculous charade. He looked at the jury, who looked skeptical. Nevertheless he said to Frizer, "Very well, you may step down. I would hear from the witnesses now. Mr. Poley, please stand before the jury. Is this what happened? You must tell the truth, upon your life."

Poley was in his element. He was a practiced liar – his life had depended upon it more than once. His role in the Babington Plot had led to the execution of a consecrated queen. He knew what to do.

"Coroner Danby, upon my word, Frizer here speaks the truth. Marlowe was crazed, I say. He was desperately worried about appearing before the Star Chamber. He had escaped it once, but felt that this would be his final hour. All day he kept talking about the Chamber – he never really got down to our business. I must admit we were becoming annoyed with him – my employer is out a great deal of money and Marlowe knew something of it, but wouldn't say. So we ate our supper without him – he said he wasn't hungry, just tired, which is why he was lying on the bed. Frizer here, who was sitting at the table on a bench between Skeres and me, said over his shoulder to Marlowe, "Well, I expect you won't have to worry about money much longer where you are going. The Star Chamber will be the end of you yet." With that, Marlowe leaped off the bed and took Frizer's dagger. He shouted, 'Aye, but I'll take at least one of you cozeners with me.' And then it was like Frizer said. Marlowe slashed Frizer's head twice, then Frizer got his knife back and stabbed Marlowe in the eye. That was that."

Poley looked at the jury. They still looked skeptical. Nicholas Draper, gentleman from Deptford, asked to speak. "Do you mean to say, sir, that this Morley didn't even use his own knife to attack Frizer? And what of you and Skeres? Why didn't you come to Frizer's aid? You were sitting on either side of him, so he couldn't get away, and simply sat there while the other two were in mortal combat? Come, sir, who could believe such a tale?

Danby cursed under his breath. Who indeed? The fools! What a ridiculous story. The queen would be displeased.

Poley's eyes glittered. "Well you might ask, sir. I know it is incredible, but that is what happened. You see, it all happened so fast. Marlowe was practiced with a knife – he had been imprisoned for violence before, in London. His temper is well known, in London. We knew to handle him carefully, but never thought he would kill us. You didn't see the crazed look in his eye. He was a desperate man – knew his end was near. He had nothing to lose, and had hate in his heart. You know he was an atheist? Talked about it that day, too. I daren't repeat what he said, but I know his soul, or what was left of it, is in hell now."

The word "atheist" had done its job. The jurors were convinced of Marlowe's guilt, and therefore Frizer's innocence. They heard Skere's testimony, which reiterated what Frizer and Poley had said, and announced their verdict – Ingrim Frizer was innocent of murder on the grounds of self-defense.

Danby breathed a sign of relief. He thanked the jury and dismissed them. He then turned to Poley and Skeres. "You may leave. The jury has accepted your testimony. The queen thanks you both for your service."

Poley grinned wolfishly, and bowed. "Indeed, Coroner Danby, it was our pleasure." He winked at Frizer, and he and Skeres went to the wharf to wait for darkness.

Danby said to Frizer, "Right, you must go with the constable here. He will detain you while I write my report. Then I will escort you back to London where you will remain in jail until you receive the queen's pardon."

He sat down to business and wrote with purpose. Danby emphasized the fact that Frizer had acted in self-defense – wrote it in the report no less than three times. He took pains over the document, as Lord Burghley had instructed him to leave a convincing account. Danby didn't know why Marlowe was held in such high regard by Her Majesty, but it wasn't for him to question. When he was finished writing, he added his seal, collected Frizer and returned to London.

The body of Christopher Marlowe, London's foremost playwright, friend of Sir Thomas Walsingham and Sir Walter Ralegh, trusted agent of Queen Elizabeth, and one of the most brilliant minds of the time, was buried that same day, in the crowded graveyard of St. Nicholas's Church, Deptford, in an unmarked grave next to many other anonymous corpses.

The Escape
2 June 1593

Lord of my love, to whom in vassalage
Thy merit hath my duty strongly knit,
To thee I send this written embassage
To witness duty, not to show my wit;
Duty so great, which wit so poor as mine
May make seem bare, in wanting words to show it,
But that I hope some good conceit of thine
In thy soul's thought (all naked) will bestow it;
Till whatsoever star that guides my moving
Points on me graciously with fair aspect,
And puts apparel on my tottered loving,
To show me worthy of [thy] sweet respect:
Then may I dare to boast how I do love thee,
Till then, not show my head where thou mayst prove me.

- William Shakespeare, Sonnet 26

The trip north to Scotland was uneventful. Robert Poley skillfully maneuvered his way through the border, as he had done many times before. Christopher thought about all he was leaving behind – his theatre, his friends, his home. But at least he had his life. For that he was eternally grateful to Thomas Walsingham, his friend and patron, who had the means, both financial and political, to save Christopher's life.

He knew now how foolish he had been. His arrogance had cost him almost everything. Christopher had underestimated Archbishop Whitgift's wrath. Now he had to start a new life, in a foreign country. He wondered whether he would ever see England again.

As the two men headed north, Poley spoke. "Just as planned. You have no doubt been buried. I wonder who was at your funeral?"

"I expect no one. As I was hiding on the dock I heard two townsfolk talking about a London playwright who had died of the plague in their fair city of Deptford, although there was some confusion about whether he might have killed someone first. They said the constable promised a quick burial, regardless of how the poor sod had died. Yes, I expect I was buried quickly."

When they stopped for the night, Christopher unpacked his bag, which contained a few clothes and a sheaf of papers. For several years now he had been turning his thoughts and feeling into sonnets. He had started soon after graduating from Cambridge. There had been an unpleasant episode with a woman, whom he had loved but who had proved false. She had turned instead to a young man whom Christopher had jokingly idealized as the perfect man. The youth was beautiful but vain and foolish, and deceitful. Christopher selected a fresh sheet and began to write.

This sonnet he "addressed" to Thomas Walsingham, the man who had risked his position, his fortune and his life to help his friend. The bond between the two men was forged by mutual respect and admiration – kindred, enlightened spirits who were fighting ignorance and superstition – and the bond superseded personal risk. Christopher knew Thomas would never betray him, as Christopher would never betray Thomas. He owed Thomas his life. Time and again Christopher would record his promise in a sonnet, pledging his loyalty, gratitude and friendship.

The next day he sailed for Italy.

The Writ
15 June 1593

Elizabeth by the grace of God of England France & Ireland Queen Defender of the Faith &c To our well-beloved William Danby, Gentleman, Coroner of our household, greeting.

We command you to send the tenor of the indictment aforesaid with every-thing touching it and whatsoever names the parties aforesaid in that indictment are known by, to us in our Chancery under your seal distinctly & openly without delay, & with this writ. Witness myself at Westminster on the 15th day of June in the year of our reign the thirty-fifth.

- Writ of Certiorari[xiii]

Burghley needed to act fast. Whitgift was making inquiries into Marlowe's death. Burghley wrote an order under the queen's name to Coroner Danby.

***

"What do you mean I am to stop investigating this ridiculous ruse? Do you really think I believe such a tale? I do not. Marlowe is ordered to appear before the Star Chamber and suddenly dies, in some backwater village? Why, the inquest is clearly faked. And now the queen wishes to control the investigation herself? Why would she have an interest in this matter? Who is she protecting, and why?" Whitgift stared at Robert Cecil, who looked back unblinking.

"Lord Archbishop, I could not say. To question the queen's orders would be treason." The implication hung in the air.

Whitgift slammed his hand on a table. He didn't trust himself to speak, so he remained silent. How he hated this disfigured man, this affront to God's perfection. Whitgift resented Lord Burghley's influence over the queen, and now it looked as if Burghely's son felt he exercised the same power.

Cecil said smoothly, "Lord Archbishop, you are most wise. The queen herself has reservations about these proceedings, which is why she has issued this writ. Evidence of any wrongdoings will be presented before her eyes, and her eyes only. Her Majesty herself will take care of this matter."

Archbishop Whitgift seethed. He knew the queen tolerated that insufferable Circle. Ralegh had once been a favorite, and it appeared she was still protecting him. If allowed to investigate, Whitgift felt sure he would be able to follow Marlowe to Ralegh, but he had been bested by none other than the queen herself.

"Very well. I will abide her Majesty's wishes. I wash my hands of the matter. As far as I am concerned, Christopher Marlowe is dead. The world is well rid of him – one less atheist. I do not doubt that one way or the other, he can be found in hell."

The Pardon
28 June 1593

We therefore moved by piety have pardoned the same Ingram ffrisar the breach of our peace which pertains to us against the said Ingram for the death above mentioned & grant to him our firm peace. In testimony &c Witness the Queen at Kewe on the 28th day of June.

- The Royal Pardon of Ingram Frizer[xiv]

The queen received William Cecil, Lord Burghley, in her chambers. "Well, what news do you bring? Our young gentleman Thomas Walsingham has been up to more intrigue. How fares our fleeing poet?"

"Your Majesty, our poet is safe. However, we must cover his tracks, and shield those who helped him escape from Archbishop Whitgift."

The queen regarded the man before her. "Lord Burghley, I understand that you have had disagreements, shall we say, with Archbishop Whitgift. But you understand that the archbishop is a trusted servant of the crown. I need his support to keep the Puritans contained, and he has done a masterful job. I don't have to tell you that religious extremists are a threat to the Crown. I will not tolerate the social unrest. The archbishop knows this and has acted accordingly. I am not pleased with this deception, but I am loath to lose one of my best informers, and my best playwright. We must settle this matter quickly and never speak of it again."

Lord Burghley bowed deeply. "Yes, your Majesty, I understand completely. I bring Coroner

Danby's report of the incident in Deptford. It proves interesting reading. Shall I?"

"By all means. I am intrigued."

The report was written in Latin but Lord Burghley translated as he read.

The queen was silent for a moment. Then she gave a short laugh. "Coroner Danby cannot be serious. Who ever would believe such an account? To think that one of the most brilliant minds of our time – a man under arrest and soon to be fighting for his life before the Star Chamber – would attack a man over the payment of a meal. It is too ridiculous! And that Marlowe attacked this Frizer from behind, with Frizer's own knife, with the other two men on either side of Frizer doing nothing? And somehow, this Frizer, who couldn't get away because of the other two hemming him in, somehow managed to turn around, retrieve his own knife and stab Marlowe in the eye? It is preposterous!"

"Your Majesty, I know the account is unbelievable, yet the jury believed it. Robert Poley is a masterful actor and convinced the jury of Frizer's innocence. Frizer has been in jail since the event but awaits your pardon, as planned. Sir Thomas is eager to have his servant back."

"Very well, I will pardon the poor wretch. He has served his master well, by risking the hangman for another of Walsingham's servants."

"Your Majesty, Christopher Marlowe is much more to Thomas Walsingham than a mere servant. They have worked together in my employ, risking their lives to serve you. They are bound by trust, respect and friendship. Walsingham's patronage has inspired Marlowe to create plays the likes of which the world has never seen. Mark my words, your Majesty, the world will remember Christopher Marlowe."

"And yet he is done, gone, dead to the world. He has written only a handful of plays, wonderful as they might be. He will not write any more."

"I believe Marlowe will continue writing, even from the grave. He has a gift, a desire, a genius that cannot be stopped. Whitgift will not deny the world Marlowe's talents. We live in a different world now, one that is alive with new knowledge and ideas. England has taken her rightful place as leader of this new world, with Your Majesty as her queen. Marlowe is not done - he is only beginning."

"Well, he must never come back. Once I sign Frizer's pardon, Marlowe must remain dead. I will have no scandal upsetting my court, nor risk the good archbishop's vengeance. How will Marlowe's new plays reach our court?"

"I believe a plan was formed in Deptford."

"Good. I do so enjoy the court's entertainments – they amuse me."

Queen Elizabeth signed the pardon Lord Burghley put before her. It was an almost exact duplicate of Coroner Danby's inquest, restating virtually word for word Frizer's actions and innocence. The queen gave a wry smile. "This must be the fastest pardon I have ever signed. Many poor victims linger for years in our prisons."

Lord Burghley bowed. "Thank you, your Majesty. Sir Thomas will be most grateful."

Immediately upon leaving the queen's chamber, Lord Burghley returned to his rooms and called for a messenger. "Take this packet to London at once. It contains several important documents that need immediate attention." The packet contained Ingram Frizer's pardon from the queen and a letter to his son Robert Cecil, instructing him to place the coroner's inquest in the Public Records Office in such a way that the inquest wouldn't see the light of day for many years, if ever.

The packet also contained a warrant for Richard Cholmeley's arrest. Lord Burghley had had enough of that fool. Cholmeley had played an instrumental role in jeopardizing one of Burghley's most valuable spies. Drury's letter had been sufficient to lead to Cholmeley's arrest. How ironic, thought Burghley, one spy released from prison, one sent in. The wheels of justice, how they turn. Richard Cholmeley was arrested that very day and never heard from again.

**Part IV
EXILE
1593 – 1623**

The Heir
12 June 1593

Vilia miretur vulgus; mihi flavus Apollo
Pocula Castalia plena ministret aqua.

> - Printed on title page of *Venus and Adonis*,
> by William Shakespeare

Let base conceited wits admire vile things,
Fair Phoebus lead me to the Musus' springs.

> - The same lines of Ovid's *Amores*,
> translated by Christopher Marlowe

Richard Field stared at the printing press. He waited impatiently for his visitor, with whom he had requested a meeting. Field had an important job to do, in fact several important jobs. One of them was to print the poem of a dead man. Christopher Marlowe had written *Venus and Adonis* some three years previously, when he also penned sonnets to the earl of Southampton for Lord Burghley. Marlowe had been working on a new version of the poem at Thomas Walsingham's house in Chislehurst, when he was arrested, then killed in Deptford. That was the official story. Field knew the real story, or at least part of it.

Upon arriving in London in the mid-1580s from his hometown of Stratford-on-Avon, Field had become an apprentice and eventual owner of a printing business. He also became a Freethinker. His first official job was to print Lord Burghley's "Copy of a Letter Sent out of England to Don Bernardin Mendoza" in 1588. Those were heady times, with the threat of the Spanish Armada looming over England. The following year Field dedicated a work to Lord Burghley and a bond was forged. Burghley saw in Field a man with a good head on his shoulders, a man who could be trusted. He came to Field with an important task – find a discreet man, an ambitious man, a man who could be trusted with a secret in exchange for a lifetime of financial security. Field knew of such a man, a man from his hometown of Stratford who was looking for work in the big city of London. That man's name was William Shakespeare.

Shakespeare sought out Field upon his arrival in London. William knew that his old friend Richard had established himself as a printer in London. Maybe Richard could use an apprentice? Jobs were scarce in Stratford, and William had to support his growing family. He had come to London, as thousands before him, to seek his fortune. As it turned out, Richard did not need an apprentice, but William left the address of the lodging house where he was staying. It was to this address that Richard sent a messenger requesting William come to the print shop to discuss an important business opportunity.

Through the shop window, Field saw Shakespeare approaching. He opened the door. "Welcome, William. Thank you for coming. We have much to discuss."

"Thank you, Richard. I must say I am interested. Your note has made me hopeful that I may find employment here in London."

"Please come into my back room. What I have to say is for your ears alone." William followed Richard past the presses into a small room at the back of the

112

shop. Richard motioned William to a chair and shut the door.

"What I am about to say can never be repeated, even if you do not agree to the arrangement. I have asked you here because you and I have known each other since childhood. We have been friends, as have our parents. I know that you left your wife and children in Stratford and are in need of employment to support them. I also know that your father has spent all the family's money and sold your mother's property that she brought with her to the marriage. There is nothing left for you back in Stratford. I know you to be quiet and reserved, and ambitious. What I am offering you is a business opportunity that will provide means of supporting yourself and your family for the rest of your lives. But with security comes risk, a risk that could cost you your life."

William stared at his old friend. What kind of business was Richard running here, and what had William stumbled on to? His mouth went dry and he cleared his throat. "Come now, Richard, what is all this? I do but seek honest employment, not intrigue. Do you mean for me to do something dishonest? I do not wish trouble from the authorities."

"The authorities are in agreement with this arrangement. I will not tell you who, but a member of the queen's court has requested me to find someone for this job. I thought of you, but I may have been wrong."

"No, please, do not think so. I simply grew frightened at your tone. I am interested in hearing more of this business."

"As I said, your life depends on your discretion, whether you say yes or no. The fact that you are sitting in this room right now has committed you to a lifetime of secrecy. The people who have asked for my help have the ability to ruin us both, and by ruin I mean imprisonment or death. It doesn't matter which to them as long as they protect their secret. However, I believe you will find that the opportunity is worth the risk, and I believe that you will be able to fulfill the terms of the deal. The terms are thus." Richard looked steadily at William, who braced himself for the monumental terms that could lead to his salvation or his destruction. Richard continued. "You will be paid, handsomely and for the rest of your life, for the use of your name, and your name shall be printed on plays written by another man."

William stared at Richard and waited for him to continue. After several moments of silence William tried to laugh but failed. "Come now, Richard, surely there must be more. All this fuss over the use of my name? Why? Who will be writing the plays? Why can't he use his own name? Who is he trying to deceive?"

Richard held up a hand. "The less you know about this business the better. In time you may come to know more details, but for now, all you must know is that your name will be printed on works you did not write, and you will be paid for your silence. As I said before, I know you to be a discrete, ambitious man who is in need of money. I hope you will agree to these vital but not too difficult terms."

Silence descended. Richard could see William fighting an inner battle. He knew he had scared William, but the man had to know the risks. Finally, William asked in a low voice, "How long must I keep this secret?"

"Until your dying day. You must tell no one, not your wife, not your children, not your townsmen.

Whatever happens, you must not speak of this arrangement, or you will lose all. What say you?"

"Can I think on it? It is a big decision, not to be taken lightly."

"I'm sorry, my friend, I must know now. I have printed a poem, which will serve to introduce a "new" poet, even though the poem was written by someone else. I simply need to add a name to the dedication and tip it into the volume. The title page has no author. If you do not agree to the terms, I must find another man."

"What is the poem, and who wrote it?"

"It is called *Venus and Adonis*, and the author is Christopher Marlowe."

"Marlowe! The playwright? Wasn't he just killed in Deptford? They thought it was the plague but now people are saying he was stabbed. I don't understand. How can a dead man write poems, and plays?"

Richard looked his confused friend steadily in the eye. At the very least William had to know this much of the secret. "Dead men cannot write poems and plays, William, you must know that." He paused, then continued. "The poem will be dedicated to the earl of Southampton."

William's mouth fell open. "You cannot be serious. How ridiculous! Who would ever dream of a nobody like me dedicating my first piece to the earl of Southampton. Why, he would have my ears cut off to be so bold."[xv]

"It is not for you to question decisions that are far beyond your role in this matter." Field knew the dedication was part of the plan to "bury" Christopher Marlowe and bring to life the name under which

Marlowe would continue to write. "Are you interested in my proposal or not?"

Slowly William's reluctance turned to acceptance. Richard saw something else in his eyes – determination. "Have no fear, Richard, I can keep this secret. For the past seven years, since I left Stratford, I have kept my own counsel. I have sent money home to my family as often as I can, but they don't know where to find me. The less my father knows of my whereabouts, the better. He cannot pay the fines imposed by the town, from his illegal wool trading to his absence from church to being bound over for threatening a citizen of Stratford. I tell you, Richard, times have been hard for the Shakespeares of Stratford." William squared his shoulders and held out his hand. "I will gladly accept money for my name, and my silence. I am your partner."

The Continent
1593-1596

When in disgrace with Fortune and men's eyes,
I all alone beweep my outcast state.

- William Shakespeare, Sonnet 29

Christopher did not waste any time when he arrived in Italy. He absorbed the culture and embraced the literature created during the Italian Renaissance. He used many northern Italian sources for new plays – *The Taming of the Shrew, Two Gentlemen of Verona*, and *Much Ado About Nothing* all had plots derived from northern Italian influences. Christopher also incorporated the Italian influence into much of his previous material. He expanded on "Hero and Leander" to produce *Romeo and Juliet, The Jew of Malta* became *The Merchant of Venice*. Not only did he reuse plots, but also he often lifted phrases or entire passages from his old works and put them in his new plays.[xvi]

Italy, along with his own traumatic experiences, had a great influence on Christopher's work. His plays matured, became less high-handed, more humble, as he explored human frailty. The Italian influence softened Christopher and his plays. The characters were deeper, as was the language. The effect was magical.

The plays were sent back to London and delivered to William Shakespeare. In order to further cover Christopher's tracks, Lord Burghley and Thomas Walsingham had created a new players' company called the Chamberlain's Men to produce Christopher's plays. Creating confusion within the theatre world at that time had not been hard to do. The theatres were closed between spring 1593 and summer 1594 because of the plague. The players took their companies on tours of the country, both to avoid the plague and to make a living. When they returned to the city, James Burbage, a veteran theatre man, headed the new company. Thomas Walsingham felt that the Admiral's Men should not perform the plays written by Christopher in exile, since his plays had been so closely associated with that company for so many years. James had two sons - Cuthbert who helped manage the company, and Richard, who became the lead actor. Christopher wrote many wonderful parts for the talented actor, just as he had written parts for Edward Alleyn. The audience loved the new plays, making the Chamberlain's Men one of the most successful acting companies in London. As part of the deal, Thomas Walsingham purchased a share of the company for William Shakespeare, who grew rich off entrance fees. Thomas made it clear, however, that William did not own the shares outright, and upon William's death, the shares would revert back to Thomas. William agreed to all the terms put before him.

The Judgment
1597

'Tis better to be vile than vile esteemed

- William Shakespeare, Sonnet 121

Thomas Beard had known Christopher Marlowe at Cambridge when they were both students studying for holy orders. Marlowe turned his back on the Church, while Beard became a Puritan minister. Beard had suspected Marlowe to be an atheist back in their school days, and his suspicions were confirmed when Marlowe had died an atheist's death four years previously. It was time to use his death to strengthen the Puritan's message – that playmakers were the Devil's messengers on earth. To that end Thomas Beard wrote *The Theatre of God's Judgment*.[xvii]

Beard had heard accounts of Marlowe's death from various sources. He knew none to be very reliable but they suited his purpose. He wasn't necessarily interested in the truth; he had a message to deliver – that atheist playmakers like Christopher Marlowe got what they deserved - a violent, painful death.

The Puritans were on the rise. Ever since Henry VIII had broken from Rome and made himself head of the church of England, Protestants made great strides in removing the pope from people's lives. Puritans wanted to go farther – they wanted to erase all signs of the Roman Church. They felt that Queen Elizabeth and her Archbishop Whitgift were too soft on Catholics, and they openly criticized the government for being too lenient. This, of course, enraged Elizabeth and angered Whitgift. The Puritans, however, continued on their mission. Eradicate the enemies of God – the Catholics, the nonbelievers, the playmakers. They went after Christopher Marlowe with a vengeance.

The Theatre of God's Judgments was the first of many Puritan accounts to vilify Christopher Marlowe. Some versions of his purported death were more accurate than others. They all had one purpose – to use Christopher Marlowe to prove the case that playmaking was the Devil's handiwork. The Puritans' goal? Destroy the theatre in London. By 1642 they succeeded, and all London theatres were shut down for over a decade.

The Treasury
1598

So the sweete wittie soule of Ovid lives in mellifluous & hony-tongued Shakespeare, witnes his Venus and Adonis, his Lucrece, his sugred Sonnets among his private friends, &c....As Plautus and Seneca are accounted the best for Comedy and Tragedy among the Latines, so Shakespeare among ye English is the most excellent in both kinds for the stage; for Comedy, witnes his Gentlemen of Verona, his Errors, his Love labors lost, his Love labours wonne, his Midsummers night dreame & his Merchant of Venice: for Tragedy, his Richard the 2, Richard the 3, Henry the 4, King Iohn, Titus Andronicus, and his Romeo and Iuliet.

- Francis Meres, *Palladis Tamia, or Wit's Treasury*[xviii]

    Commissioned to write the second of four literary source books in the series called *Wits Commonwealth*, Francis Meres was a busy man. After reading *Politeuphuia*, the first book of the collection, Meres felt he could do better. Instead of simply writing a series of pithy scholarly lessons, he decided to treat his readers to his knowledge of the contemporary literary world. The number of poets was impressive, and Meres set about listing the most noteworthy. He decided to compare each contemporary author with a classical poet, an added twist that was sure to impress his audience.

    Meres was at his desk when he heard a knock at the chamber door. A servant entered to say he had a visitor wishing an audience. Meres sighed heavily and put his quill down. Sometimes the Lord saw fit to try his patience.

The visitor introduced himself as Ingram Frizer. "Forgive me, sir, for the intrusion. I understand you are working on a book. I have some information you may want to include."

Meres looked the man up and down. "Indeed I am working on a book of literary note. I am calling it *Pallidis Tamia*, or *Wits Treasury*. In fact, I was just writing about Christopher Marlowe, that unfortunate degenerate who met his death at the hands of a rival in some love affair. Such a pity – he showed great promise. But God does as He sees fit. What information, pray tell, could you supply me that would be of any use to my book?"

Frizer's face twitched in humor – rumors of Marlowe's death ran rampant. "Sir, I come on behalf of my master Sir Thomas Walsingham. Here is his note of introduction. He is the patron of William Shakespeare, the playwright. You have heard of him?"

"Yes, of course. I will be listing Shakespeare as a popular poet of the day, along with several others."

"Sir, it is my master's wish that you write favorably of his playwright, so that the world will know Shakespeare for the genius that he is. Your book, no doubt, will have a large audience, since you are held in such high regard."

Meres swelled visibly. He knew himself to be a man of importance. He had a bachelor's degree from Cambridge, a master's degree from Oxford and he had been commissioned for this important work. Nevertheless, he hesitated.

"I would treat all the poets of today the same – I show no favoritism. I hardly know this Shakespeare, and I certainly would not hold him above the likes of Sir Philip Sidney, may God rest his soul."

"Sir, my master is most insistent. I have here portions of plays by William Shakespeare. You can see for yourself that they are most excellent and of the highest quality. In addition, I have some of the sonnets that have been circulating at Gray's Inn. These were, of course, intended for the amusement of the young gentlemen of the Inn, but my master thought you might mention them in your book. The quality, as you can see, is quite extraordinary, much on the same level as Sir Philip Sidney."

Meres took the stack of papers Frizer handed him. The papers included a list of twelve plays written by Shakespeare, several loose sheets of fair copies from the plays (but not the complete plays, Meres noted) and the fifteen sonnets written for the "Prince of Purpoole" William Hatcliffe at Gray's Inn (a barristers' association).

Frizer continued. "Sir, my master, as I have said, is very interested in establishing his poet's reputation as a master playwright. Sir Thomas believes Shakespeare to be the best playwright that has ever lived, or that will live. He hopes you will be of the same opinion, and will help convince the Christian world of the same." With this, Frizer laid a small pouch on Meres's writing table.

Francis Meres eyed the pouch warily. Could this be a bribe? "What would your master have me do? Put Shakespeare above all others? I am not that familiar with his work. Of course I have read his *Venus and Adonis* and his *Lucrece* – the poems have been printed many times over. But you have just handed me these plays, which have not yet been published, and I never laid eyes on the sonnets, since as you said, they have circulated only among the gentlemen at Gray's Inn."

"My master believes that once you read Shakespeare's work, you will see him for the genius he is, and that you will have no qualms about placing him above all others. My master simply wishes for you to list the plays in your book, by name, and mention the sonnets – they are most skillfully written. You will find that Shakespeare is most versatile – he writes poetry, comedy, and tragedy. Few poets today can say the same."

"Yes, well, I will be the judge of that." Meres rang for his servant to show Frizer out. "Please thank your master for supplying me with this information. I do not doubt he will be pleased with my efforts on behalf of his poet."

After Frizer left, Meres hefted the pouch. He opened it and poured the contents into his palm. The amount of money in his hand felt good. Meres poured the coins back into the pouch, set it down on the table and took up the sheets of paper Frizer had left. As Meres began to read, he felt better about the pouch on his writing table. The plays were good, and the sonnets were the best he had ever read. This Shakespeare truly was superior. Meres decided his conscience could rest.

The Rival Poet
1598

Then if he thrive and I be cast away,
The worst was this, my love was my decay.

- William Shakespeare, Sonnet 80

Thomas Walsingham was getting married. Christopher knew the perfect wedding gift – his beautiful poem *Hero and Leander,* which he had been working on at Scadbury Manor at the time of his arrest five years ago. It was now in the hands of his friend and fellow Freethinker Edward Blount. Christopher wanted Blount to publish the poem and dedicate it to Thomas Walsingham as a wedding gift.

The poem was duly published, and the printing included what Blount thought a very clever dedication. He fell just short of saying that Christopher was alive and well.[xix] Only those who knew the truth would think anything of the hints in the dedication, and they wouldn't be talking.

Shortly after publication, Blount received a summons from Sir Thomas. Naturally he expected to be thanked and praised for his efforts. He was partially right.

Thomas was most cordial. "Pray be seated. I like the poem exceedingly well. However, I am wondering if it could be completed."

"Completed, my lord? I do not understand. As we both know, dear Christopher is dead. I miss him still. I cannot see how he can complete his lovely poem."

"Of course, dear Christopher cannot complete his poem, but another poet can."

Blount felt a stab of apprehension. He did not like where this was heading, and he knew Christopher would be angry. "Another poet, my lord? Whom did you have in mind?"

"George Chapman, of course. A stout fellow and wonderful poet. As you know I have been his patron for a number of years. I thought he could finish the poem and dedicate it to my bride. I will have it beautifully bound and present it to her as a wedding gift."

"My lord, what a wonderful thought. It's just that, well, one could say that the poem is complete and does not need finishing. I believe Christopher would have wanted it left untouched."

"Nonsense. You said yourself in the dedication to me that the poem was unfinished. I'm sure Christopher wouldn't mind if a poet of Chapman's talent finished his work – he would be honored."

"My lord, please reconsider. Poets are temperamental. I'm sure Christopher would object – if he could."

Thomas became frosty. "Be that as it may, I will ask Chapman to finish the poem and dedicate it to the soon-to-be Lady Walsingham. You can leave the temperamental poet to me."

"Very well, my lord. I will await the finished poem." Blount left Scadbury with a heavy heart. He knew Christopher would be furious, and he was right.

***

Christopher was, in fact, devastated. When word reached him that George Chapman had added three stanzas to "Hero and Leander," Christopher exploded. Why, the poem was now more Chapman's than his! After all these years, to be betrayed by his most trusted friend, who now valued the work of another over his. Wasn't his life already ruined? To be cast off by the one person whom Christopher felt would remain true.

As always, Christopher expressed his deepest feelings in words. He wrote sonnet after sonnet, fourteen in all, revealing his anguish, bitterness and resentment. It was bad enough that another man's name was on his plays, but now another man would receive credit for his beautiful poem, a poem that far surpassed his first attempt of "Venus and Adonis." And all the attacks that were coming from those wretched Puritans, spreading lies about his death and character. It was almost more than Christopher could bear.

The Pilgrim
1599

The
PASSIONATE
Pilgrime.
By W. Shakespeare.
AT LONDON
Printed for W. Iaggard, and are
To be sold by W. Leake, at the Grey-
Hound in Paules Churchyard.
1599

- Title page of *The Passionate Pilgrim*

William Jaggard knew he was taking a risk – publishing a book of poems by William Shakespeare that Shakespeare had not written. But the risk was small, and calculated. Jaggard knew William Shakespeare would not object to his name being put on works that he had not written. He never did.

A small group of men knew the circumstances surrounding the plays of William Shakespeare. They either knew or suspected that Shakespeare was not the true author. A still smaller group knew the name of the actual author. Jaggard suspected, but he didn't know. What he did know was that William Shakespeare's name was for sale, and it sold well. Audiences packed the theatres to watch Shakespeare's plays.

Jaggard assembled a collection of poems, which included passages from Shakespeare's recently published play *Love's Labor's Lost*, two of his sonnets that had been circulating around London's literary circle, and fifteen other poems, including "The

Passionate Shepherd to his Love." The poem reached Jaggard in a circuitous fashion, so the text was somewhat altered. In fact, Jaggard obtained most of the poems second-hand. Their authors knew nothing of the upcoming publication (at least two of the authors were dead) and therefore did not have the opportunity to edit their works, let alone give permission for inclusion. The result – a very short booklet containing twenty poems of varying quality and accuracy and dubious authorship. It did, in fact, sell very well and went into several printings.

The following year, *England's Helicon* was published. It was an anthology of England's finest literature, compiled by John Flasket. It included, among others, works by Sir Philip Sidney, Robert Greene, and Edmund Spenser. The *Helicon* also included "The Passionate Shepherd to his Love,"[xx] accurately attributed to Christopher Marlowe, and "The Nymph's Reply,"[xxi] a poem by Sir Walter Ralegh that matched Marlowe's line for line. The text of the "Shepherd" was superior in quality to Jaggard's printed version, and gave proper credit to its true author Christopher Marlowe. The perception at the time was that Jaggard printed *The Passionate Pilgrim* using William Shakespeare's name without permission. Despite this, William Shakespeare, an extremely litigious man who had sued and been sued on many occasions in his hometown of Stratford, never uttered one word of complaint against Jaggard for the unauthorized use of his name on *The Passionate Pilgrim*.

***

Christopher Marlowe, on the other hand, was livid. It was the final straw. He began work on another play, this one revealing the truth.

He contacted Thomas Thorpe, who was just about to publish Christopher's translation of *Lucan's First Book*. Thorpe was discreet and trustworthy. Christopher knew his new play wouldn't pass Lord Burghley's censors – it came too close to revealing the identity of the author of the Shakespeare plays. But he had to try.

The Fury
4 August 1600

When a man's verses cannot be understood, nor a man's good wit seconded with the forward child understanding, it strikes a man more dead than a great reckoning in a little room.

- William Shakespeare, *As You Like It*

Christopher speaks through the character Touchstone, whose name means "truth." *As You Like It* is liberally sprinkled with allusions that William Shakespeare was an imposter. The "great reckoning in a little room" – very few people knew anything of the Coroner's Inquest, which described the dispute over the bill in Dame Eleanor Bull's house. That miserable Thomas Beard thought Christopher had been killed in London by accidentally plunging his own knife into his head. The people who understood the passage understood the danger.

Christopher then explicitly states that he is William and William is he – they are one in the same. In the play, William is a country bumpkin, living in the Forest of Arden (Arden was Shakespeare's mother's maiden name). Christopher then warns William to stay away, to stop putting his name on Christopher's plays, or Christopher will kill him, figuratively or possibly literally.

The play was a cry of anguish, a desperate attempt to regain a lost reputation and a lost life. Christopher knew it wouldn't pass into publication, even if Thorpe tried to sneak it past the Circle. Thomas Walsingham had too much to lose. He was newly married and newly knighted. He couldn't allow Christopher to come back – not until Archbishop Whitgift and Queen Elizabeth were dead.

***

Thomas Thorpe was a complicated man. He had agreed to help Christopher get his damaging play published, and he couldn't help hinting at trouble for the Circle should this play get published. He knew Christopher was planning on returning to London, and that he had three or four plays he would be trying to sell at St. Paul's, bypassing Shakespeare at the Globe. Christopher had promised the most damaging play to Thomas Thorpe, a play that would reveal William Shakespeare as an imposter.

Thorpe had recently obtained the rights to Marlowe's translation of *Lucan's First Book*, from Edward Blount, a fellow Circle member. Thorpe publish *Lucan* and included a dedication to Blount, hinting that Christopher was back in London and had several plays ready for publication – plays that would cause Edward Blount and the other Freethinkers a great deal of trouble.[xxii]

Not only did Thomas Thorpe succeed in boasting to Edward Blount about his future plans, he also succeeded in preventing the publication of the very play Christopher meant to uncover the truth. Christopher sold his plays, in disguise, but failed to get them printed. On 4 August 1600, three "Shakespeare" plays were submitted to the Stationer's Register – *Much Ado About Nothing*, *Henry V* and *As You Like It*. All three were "stayed" – that is, prevented from publication. After the Circle had a chance to review the plays, they allowed *Henry V* to be passed 14 August and *Much Ado* on 23 August 1600. *As You Like It* would not be published, printed, or performed for almost a quarter of a century.

The Reconciliation
c. 1601-1602

That you were once unkind befriends me now,
And for that sorrow, which I then did feel,
Needs must I under my transgression bow,
Unless my nerves were brass or hammered steel.
For if you were by my unkindness shaken,
As I by yours, you've passed a hell of time;
And I, a tyrant, have no leisure taken
To weigh how once I suffered in your crime.
O! that our night of woe might have remembered
My deepest sense, how hard true sorrow hits,
And soon to you, as you to me, then tendered
The humble salve, which wounded bosoms fits!
But that your trespass now becomes a fee;
Mine ransoms yours, and yours must ransom me.

- William Shakespeare, Sonnet 120

The two men met at Scadbury Manor. Christopher dressed as a Frenchman. His disguise had kept him safe for many years. He was the first to speak.

"You look well, Thomas. Marriage agrees with you."

"You look terrible. Exile disagrees with you. For that, and for what I have done, I am truly sorry. I never meant to hurt you. I simply wanted to give Lady Walsingham a fine marriage gift. I should have left your poem alone. Please accept my apologies."

"My friend, it is I who must apologize. I know the play was a foolish thing to do. Luckily your people stayed it. With everything that was happening, I could take no more. I never truly intended to cause you harm either. But my life is no longer my own. I thought things would be different, that somehow I could come home and have my old life back. I know now that will never happen. There is too much at stake, for all of us. I will never have my life back."

Thomas read the anguish in his friend's face. "I know life must be very difficult for you. But your plays are so very successful. The theatres are crowded every day. That must give you some measure of satisfaction."

"A small measure. No one knows it is I who wrote them. William Shakespeare's name on my plays! I thought I could live with this arrangement, but it is so much more difficult than I imagined. I cannot bear it any longer."

"Christopher, please, you know this is the only way you can continue to write plays. Shakespeare has kept his end of the bargain. He has told no one in all these years. Only a very few know, or suspect, the truth. Ben Jonson knows and put in that silly jibe in his play, but once the Circle saw it was harmless, they let the play pass."

"Which play is that? I am afraid I am not current in the London theatre."

"*Every Man Out of His Humour.* Jonson jested at Shakespeare's coat-of-arms. Somehow Jonson found out that Shakespeare's application was found to be without merit. Jonson's line 'Not without mustard. Your crest is very rare, sir,'[xxiii] hit close, but not too close. The play was stayed on the same day as *As You Like It*, but we lifted the ban soon after. Rather a good play, that."

"I do not care about Jonson's plays or Shakespeare's coat-of-arms! I want my life back and I can never have it." Christopher fell silent, then said quietly "I sometimes wish I were dead."

"Christopher, please, do not speak, or even think of such things! I know it has been difficult, but you are alive! How could death be better? I cannot imagine life without your plays – you bring so much to the theatre. Why, man, you have changed the theatre! How could you not be moved by what you have done? I am. You are the greatest playwright that has ever lived. Somehow, you will be remembered, for who you really are. I don't know how, and I don't know when, but someday the world will know who Christopher Marlowe was and what he meant to the English theatre."

Christopher looked out the window at the beautiful gardens of Scadbury. He doubted if Thomas was right but was too tired to argue. "Thank you, my friend. You give me reason to live, even if I don't want to. I won't do anything else so foolish, I promise."

"Good. Leave that to the characters in your plays. In return, I will decrease the number of times I put forth Shakespeare's name."

Thomas was good for his word. In 1598, in his *Wit's Treasury*, Francis Meres credited William Shakespeare with having written twelve plays. Between 1600 and 1623, the name William Shakespeare was used only four times to register plays.

The Darkness
1605

I have no spur To prick the sides of my intent, but only Vaulting ambition, which o'erleaps itself, And falls on th' other.

- William Shakespeare, *Macbeth*

The first five years of the new century marked several events that changed the course of history and made a tremendous impact on Christopher Marlowe's life.

In February 1601, Robert Devereux, the 2nd earl of Essex, gathered a group of supporters and rode in the streets of London against his queen. He was summarily executed 30 February 1601. His chief intelligence officer, Anthony Bacon, died within months of his master. Giordano Bruno, that heretical Italian philosopher who greatly influenced Christopher within the Circle, was burned at the stake in Italy the year before.

On 24 March 1603, after forty-five years on the throne, Queen Elizabeth passed away quietly in her sleep. Archbishop Whitgift, who attended Elizabeth on her deathbed, died less than a year later on 29 February 1604. Upon the death of Queen Elizabeth, James VI of Scotland became James I of England. He was the son of Mary Stuart, whom Elizabeth had executed in 1587. James was raised by a Scottish regent and grew up a devout Protestant. Robert Cecil was instrumental in placing James on the English throne. In return, James kept Robert on as his secretary of state.

The new king was a religious man and took a dislike to the scientific-minded Walter Ralegh and Henry Percy, the Wizard Earl. He imprisoned both Ralegh and Northumberland in the Tower of London soon after he ascended the throne. Robert Cecil, who stood to gain power when others lost it, had heavily influenced the king in this decision. Two of Christopher's strongest supporters had fallen from grace.

Thomas and Audrey Walsingham, however, did not fall. In fact, they rose to high positions in James's court. Audrey had been a lady of the bedchamber to Queen Elizabeth and the high favor carried over to the new court. Lady Walsingham had ridden to Scotland to accompany the new king and queen to England, and she and Thomas became joint holders of the office of Chief Keeper of the Queen's Wardrobe. Audrey participated in Queen Anne's masques and was awarded an annual pension of two hundred pounds by the queen.

Lady Audrey Walsingham was also the mistress, and political tool, of Robert Cecil. If Thomas Walsingham ever wanted his friend and poet to come home, Lady Walsingham and Robert Cecil dissuaded him. Christopher Marlowe was a liability and knew too many secrets that could unbalance the scales of power. Both Robert Cecil and Thomas Walsingham had a great deal to lose if the new king learned of their deception. They were determined not to let that happen. Christopher asked both, repeatedly, if he could return home. Both denied him. Christopher no longer had any hope of returning to his former life. His plays reflected this despair. Within five years he wrote four of the most compelling tragedies the world has seen. Prince Hamlet contemplated revenge and death. Othello lost his reputation and his fight against evil. King Lear lost his family and his mind. In the darkest tragedy, Macbeth and his lady, temporarily triumphant in evil, are eventually overcome by virtue and justice. Christopher's characters said what he could not say for himself.

The Sonnets
1609

Not marble, nor the gilded monuments
Of princes, shall outlive this powerful rhyme;
But you shall shine more bright in these contents

- William Shakespeare, Sonnet 55

St. Paul's was crowded as usual. The booksellers displayed their wares and customers slowly made their way through the bookstalls. Two booksellers, William Aspley and John Wright, were in deep conversation.

"Have you ever seen the like? What are we to make of this, then? Have you ever seen such a strange dedication, by the publisher no less and not the author himself? I wonder at Shakespeare. Why didn't he write the dedication himself, or at the very least, why wasn't the book dedicated to him? Who is this Mr. W.H? 'Everliving poet'? Why, the man is living, not dead. And why such a strange shape, with all the capital letters and periods? It almost seems like a code, but for what, and why?" [xxiv] William Aspley was perplexed indeed.

"Well, now, William, I don't know the answers. I have a few questions myself. Why did Thorpe print "Shake-speare," with the hyphen, not just on the title page, but on every page? I've heard Shakespeare is a false name, that the real author of all those plays and these sonnets is afraid to use his real name. Why would that be? Do you suppose he's a noble? Do you think he has something to hide?" John Wright was just as confused as his fellow bookseller. "And for that matter, have you read the sonnets? Quiet lovely, they are, but I can't tell who they're written to."

"Seems as if they are addressed to several different people, men and women, not just one "begetter." Who the devil do you think this Dark Lady is? And the Fair Youth? Seems that our Shakespeare fancies both types, if you know what I mean. He should watch himself. That kind of love is deadly – to put it in print is suicide." Aspley shook his head.

"Nay, I don't think so. You know how these poets are – when they say they love a man, they mean honor and respect. Why, even Sir Philip Sydney, may God rest his soul, wrote of loving another man in that way, and Sydney was the manliest man there ever was. I tell you, Shakespeare's plays and poems speak for themselves. I don't doubt he fancies women, all right." John Wright seemed quite convinced.

Aspley remained skeptical. "But there seem to be other people, like a rival poet and a patron who seems to have gotten Shakespeare out of some serious trouble. I tell you, I can't make it out. Why would William Shakespeare write of such things? From what I know of the man, he lives a very quiet life. Spends most of his time in that little town Stratford of his. As far as I know he doesn't have a mistress, and he hasn't been in any feuds with other authors, not like Thomas Nashe and Gabriel Harvey a few years back. That row got right nasty. But Shakespeare's always been quiet. Never a word out of him. The sonnets seem to be about a man's life, but don't seem to have anything to do with William Shakespeare's life, as far as I can tell."

"Indeed, indeed, 'tis a mystery indeed. And that poem at the end, "The Lover's Complaint" – what do you make of that? All those mistakes in print. Makes me wonder at Thomas Thorpe for being so careless, unless.... Maybe he didn't have Shakespeare look over the sheets. Maybe he just printed the poems for himself, without Shakespeare's knowing it." John Aspley grew excited at the thought.

"Well, now, William, how can that be? Surely if Thorpe stole the sonnets, Shakespeare would object. What author would allow his work to be printed without his consent and not object? They get little enough money and recognition as it is. I tell you, 'tis a puzzle, but we have these books to sell. Let's get to it."

***

Thomas Walsingham read the book with increasing horror. Christopher had done the unthinkable. He had published his sonnets, a record of his intense relationships with several people, including Thomas Walsingham. Some sonnets all but said that Christopher had faked his death, his patron (who everyone knew was Thomas Walsingham) had helped him, and that Christopher was living in anonymity and shame. Luckily for him, Christopher was back in Italy. Otherwise, Thomas might have wrung his neck. As it was, he had to act fast. He tried to buy up all the copies from the booksellers, but most had already been sold. Walsingham went straight to Thomas Thorpe.

"How dare you publish Marlowe's sonnets! You knew the risk – you have put all of us, especially me, in danger. Christopher Marlowe is dead, and he needs to stay dead. How can people read those sonnets and not know they were written by Christopher? He practically signed them. I will not lose my position or reputation – they are everything to me! And what the devil do you mean by writing such a dedication?"

Thomas Thorpe pleaded. "My lord, please hear me. I do not doubt you are angry, but I have taken precautions. Marlowe carefully arranged the sonnets as to throw confusion on the subjects. No one but you and a very few others can possibly know the identity of the people. Marlowe also wrote the dedication to add to the confusion. He hasn't even told me who Mr. W.H. is. And we printed "Shake-speare" on every page to plant the name in people's minds."

"Yes, but with that ridiculous hyphen. Who would not guess it is a pseudonym?"

"My lord, he insisted. Marlowe can only be pushed so far. Besides, you overestimate the people. I do not doubt the author's true identity will remain a secret for a generation or two, certainly after we are long dead and buried. His secret is safe, I assure you."

"Nevertheless, there will be no further printings of this book in my lifetime – do you understand? None!"

Thorpe understood. The sonnets quickly disappeared from the bookstalls and the collection was not reprinted for over thirty years.

***

Christopher understood as well. When he heard of Thomas's reaction, Christopher knew his friend and patron would no longer protect him as in the past. Thomas wanted Christopher dead, and no longer a threat. Returning was not an option. Revealing his true identity was not an option. The friendship was over. Thomas was a married man, a knight in His Majesty's court, very well placed and well rewarded. He was not going to risk losing his position, nor his wife's, over a dead man.

The Final Curtain
1612
James I's Court

As you from crimes would pardon'd be,
Let your indulgence set me free.

- Epilogue, *The Tempest*

All the courtiers and their ladies were assembled in the great hall, awaiting his Majesty James I of England and his queen Anne of Denmark. Both loved plays and the queen performed in many masques written especially for her and her ladies-in-waiting, of which Lady Audrey Walsingham was one.

The court was gathered to watch the latest play from that wonderful playwright William Shakespeare. When James ascended the throne in 1603, he became patron of the Chamberlain's Men, which became the King's Men, the company that had exclusive rights to the plays of William Shakespeare.

The play began soon after the monarch arrived. And what a play it was. Full of music – the most ever in a play from Shakespeare. And magic - both white from the wizard Prospero, based on science, rationality and divinity, and black from the sorceress Sycorax, based in the occult, destructive and terrible. And illusion – the senses were tricked in every scene. In a word, *The Tempest* was magical.

Thomas Walsingham and Robert Cecil watched the play by the king's side. As the play progressed, character traits emerged, and the two men grew uneasy. Could it be true? Were they watching a play depicting the people in Christopher Marlowe's life who had betrayed him and forced him to live out his days in exile? It seemed only too true.

Christopher wrote himself as the powerful wizard Prospero, who uses his benevolent magic to set wrongs right, and forgive those who wronged him. The usurper Alonso is William Shakespeare, mildly cunning but ineffectual and harmless. The sprite Ariel bares traces of Thomas Walsingham, whom Christopher still loves but knows to be inconsistent. The worst is saved for Robert Cecil, portrayed by a deformed monster, treacherous and cunning. While most of the lowly characters in the play speak in prose, the most hideous of them all speaks in verse. Few in the court missed the comparison, least of all Robert Cecil himself, whose hunched back earned him the nickname "pigmy" by the Queen Elizabeth when she was alive. That cursed Marlowe – would he never die?

In the last act of the play, Prospero gives a speech, which Thomas knew from Christopher's translations of Ovid, his favorite classical poet. The speech was a virtual word-for-word duplication from Medea in *Metamorphoses*, another clever sign from Christopher to his former patrons. The speech was a farewell to magic - that is, playwriting - where Prospero promises to "drown the book." Walsingham and Cecil took this to be an indication that Christopher was through writing plays, and they were right.

Although the play made the two men in court uneasy, they were relieved by the Epilogue, which was full of resignation, acceptance and forgiveness. Prospero forgives all who wronged him, and by doing so, sets himself free. The two men drew a sign of relief as the play came to a close. Christopher would not betray them to the king. He would not try to come

145

home anymore, and he would cause no further trouble. The Tempest was over.

The Will
1616
Stratford-upon-Avon

Good Friends, for Jesus' sake forbear,
To dig the bones enclosed here!
Blest be the man that spares these stones,
And curst be he that moves my bones.

- William Shakespeare's epitaph,
written by himself

William Shakespeare drew a sigh. He was tired, tired of dealing with his business and tired of the secret he had been keeping all these years. He was glad it was almost over.

Francis Collins, the lawyer from Worcester whom William had hired to draw up his will, looked up from the desk. He had been to Stratford only two months previously to draw up William's original will, but Shakespeare's daughter Judith's recent marriage to Thomas Quiney on 10 February had made necessary a few changes. What was once her dowry was now her marriage portion. "Well, the changes have been made. Judith will be provided for, but her new husband cannot break up the estate. It will be kept intact for your first male heir. I must say, I have never written so detailed a will on keeping an estate together. You have been most careful."

"You would be too, if your father had sold your family's estate little by little and left you with nothing. I mean to do better by my descendants. The name Shakespeare will be tied to this land for all eternity."

"Yes, quite. That is assuming you indeed have a male heir. The death of your son Hamnet has ended your chances of passing on your family name, but you can, in fact, pass your line indirectly through your married daughters. Now, I must ask again, are you sure you want to leave nothing to your wife but her rightful share of your property? I must say, sir, that this is most unusual."

"Mr. Collins, my wife and I have an understanding. I don't expect you to understand our relationship – few do. When I married Anne, she was three months with child – our daughter Susanna. Our twins Judith and Hamnet were born two years later, and two years after that I moved to London. I have never pretended to be a family man – Anne knew that when she married me. I saved her reputation, but I never promised to be a loving husband. If you are concerned about appearances, you can add that she is to have our marriage bed. I believe that is a customary bequest from a husband to a wife."

The lawyer raised his eyebrows slightly at Shakespeare's detachment. The will showed no emotion whatsoever, no loving words about family and friends, in fact one of the coldest wills Collins had ever written. The usual bequests had been made, the family provided for, but the will was devoid of any feelings of gratitude or love. Highly unusual for a man who wrote such moving plays that touched time and again on the very essence of the human spirit. Also unusual for that same man not to have written a eulogy upon the death in 1596 of his only son Hamnet, as other poets had. And even more unusual for one of London's foremost playwrights to have semi-literate children. The man who had created such characters as Portia, Beatrice and

Rosalind had one daughter Susanna who signed her name in a very shaky hand, and another Judith who signed with a mark. Girls were not allowed at Stratford's King Edward VI School, and Shakespeare obviously had not hired tutors for his daughters' education.

Collins knew of William Shakespeare's work as a playwright, but he never saw any indication of the trade in Shakespeare's house. The estate listed no plays, manuscripts, or books, not even a Bible. He was no expert on the theatre, but Collins assumed that a London playwright would own at least a few books. But there were none in the house, and Shakespeare did not list any in his will.[xxv]

He asked Shakespeare, "And what of your London interests? The property in Blackfriars you purchased some years ago – 1613 wasn't it? And if I remember correctly, don't you own shares in that theatre of yours – the Globe? Will you be leaving those assets to your theatre friends, the ones you have bequeathed money for rings?" Collins was referring to John Heminge and Henry Condell, who had helped William carry out the charade by transporting the play manuscripts from Marlowe to the King's Men. They had kept the secret and treated him fairly. Heminge even co-signed for the property at Blackfriars, although the act had been at Thomas Walsingham's insistence.

"I do not have any theatre shares to bequest – they have been disposed of." Thomas Walsingham had made it perfectly clear that William never owned the shares outright. He may have received the money as if he was the owner, but Walsingham controlled the shares. The arrangement had suited William perfectly. "As far as the Blackfriars property goes, I want that

149

protected for the entail as well. London may think Anne is entitled to one third of my property as her dower rights, but I don't. The house is to be held by three trustees, until it can be given to my heir. Until then, I will continue to rent it to the current tenant – the property has proved to be a sound investment."

"Have you given any thought to the future of your plays? Several people have published various forms of your plays, but you have never objected, or tried to publish the plays yourself."

"I do not care what happens to the plays. They have suited their purpose. I have lived a good life, and have provided for my family. That is all I care about."

"Very well, I have it all here. There is no need to make a fair copy of the will – your corrections have been made and this document will stand in court. Now, have you thought about your final resting place? Does your family know your wishes?"

"Yes, I will be buried here in Stratford. The other playwrights of London are all clamoring to be buried in Westminster Abbey, alongside old Chaucer. What do I care for that? I have lived in two worlds – London and Stratford. I lived in London, but my life is in Stratford. I was born here, I will die here and I will be buried here. Speaking of that, what do you think of my epitaph? I wrote it myself – should keep away the grave robbers. No one will move my bones to make way for new ones. I deserve to be treated with respect, after all I have done for this town."

Collins thought of the mere ten pounds Shakespeare left the poor of Stratford, but said nothing. "I thought your epigraph more than a little simplistic, for one of the most skilled playwrights of the day. In fact, it could have been written by a child."

The words stung William to the core. He had never cared that he had profited from another man's words, but he had taken pains over his epigraph, his message to posterity. "Well, I think it quite clever. I have, of course, written more plays than you. It stands as it is."

"Of course. I beg your pardon. I will take my leave and wish you good day." The witnesses were assembled, the will signed and the lawyer departed. With that, William was left to his thoughts.

William wandered into his garden of New Place, that impressive house bought with Thomas Walsingham's money, and thought about a great many things - about how he had succeeded where his father had failed, about the life he had chosen, or rather that had chosen him, about the strange arrangement he had made all those years ago, which had worked out exactly according to plan. He had kept his end of the bargain and profited handsomely. He cared little about the theatre life, only that he had amassed property and wealth that he would be passing on to his heir. William felt a twinge of anxiety over his heir – what if his children or grandchildren did not produce a male heir? What if all William had worked for disappeared with no trace? What if the name Shakespeare were forgotten? William shuddered at the thought. All his hopes and dreams, his life's work, all for nothing. It was more than William could bear.

He sat down on a bench in the sun. His thoughts moved to another man, Christopher Marlowe, who was the true writer of all those plays. He wondered how Marlowe felt to have someone else's name on his work. William knew Marlowe had hinted at his true identity, through some of his plays, and of course, through that whole sonnet fiasco. That had been a close call. Fortunately, Walsingham and Cecil had suppressed the dangerous documents quickly – little harm done. Still, William supposed being an anonymous playwright was better than being a dead playwright.

***

Less than a month after the revision of his will, William Shakespeare of Stratford-on-Avon died of an unknown illness on 23 April 1616 at the age of fifty-two. There was no mention of his death in London, and not a single playwright or patron attended his funeral. He was buried in Stratford, as was his wish, and his simplistic epitaph still stands, confounding his reputation as one of the most eloquent writers the world has even known.

The Folio
1623

Looke Not on his Picture, but his Booke.

- Excerpt of poem by Ben Jonson
facing the Shakespeare Folio title page.[xxvi]

Ben Jonson was well pleased. *Mr. William Shakespeare's Comedies, Histories and Tragedies* was finished. Jonson had played an instrumental role in the publication. In fact he had done most of the editing. The reason? Jonson wanted plays to be considered serious literature, the very reason he had published his own works in 1616. Even though Jonson knew William Shakespeare to be an imposter, he understood the plays were great literature and deserved to be remembered for all time. In that light, Shakespeare's folio of plays justified Jonson's works.

Several people brought the book to fruition. John Heminge and Henry Condell, two owners of the Globe Theatre and actors in the King's Men, had collected the plays, many of which had never been printed – *The Tempest, The Two Gentlemen of Verona, Measure for Measure, The Comedy of Errors, As You Like It, The Taming of the Shrew, All's Well that Ends Well, Twelfth Night, The Winter's Tale, King John, Henry VI Part I, Henry VIII, Coriolanus, Timon of Athens, Macbeth, Anthony and Cleopatra, and Cymbeline* would have disappeared without a trace if not for the publication of the folio. Ralph Crane, a professional scrivener employed by the King's Men, made fair copies from Christopher's original manuscripts for the printer. Edward Blount, because of his good reputation and involvement with "Hero and

Leander," published the book. William Jaggard printed the folio. Despite his notorious past with Shakespeare's works, Jaggard's was one of the few printing houses big enough to handle a job of such magnitude. The folio was big – twelve by fifteen inches and almost a thousand pages. It took two years to print. There were interruptions in printing and difficulty obtaining publishing rights. By November 1623 the book was ready for publication. William Jaggard died that same month and the work was brought to the Stationer's Register by his son Isaac. It sold for a pound, a sizeable sum for a sizable book

The first page of the folio contained a poem by Ben Jonson, referring to the engraving of William Shakespeare opposite the title page. Engraved by Martin Droeshout, it was a curious portrait, made under curious circumstances. Ben Jonson had planned well.

It was indeed a likeness of William Shakespeare – balding, bulbous forehead, bags under the eyes, long nose, mustache. Jonson had described him to Droeshout, who had never met Shakespeare. Jonson also gave the engraver curious instructions – William Shakespeare was to be dressed as a merchant, as he was known in Stratford. The fancy collar, shoulder crescents, intricate embroidery, taffeta doublet and gold buttons all showed Shakespeare to be a prosperous businessman. Most curious of all – Jonson requested that a distinct line run along the left side of Shakespeare's face, giving the illusion of a mask. The illusion was remarkably visible when one turned the image upside down. Droeshout wondered at these instructions but did not question them. One learned to keep one's mouth shut in these dangerous times.

***

154

Mr. William Shakespeare's Comedies, Histories, &
Tragedies of 1623, today known as the First Folio,
proved so popular that it went into three subsequent
printings – the Second Folio in 1632, the Third Folio in
1663 and the Fourth Folio in 1685. Shakespeare's plays
have not only survived for four hundred years but are
performed worldwide on a daily basis. He had a 21,000-
word vocabulary and coined some 1,500 words, many
of which are still in use today. His plays are studied in
schools and universities around the world, and books
about his life abound. All this from an uneducated man
who lived in a small village in England and died un-
mourned by the foremost literary community the world
had ever seen.

EPILOGUE

1901
Ohio, U.S.A.

In the characteristic curve of his plays Christopher Marlowe agrees with Shakespeare about as well as Shakespeare agrees with himself.

- Dr. Thomas C. Mendenhall, "A Mechanical
Solution of a Literary Problem"[xxvii]

The two women sat across from each other at a large table spread with notepaper, graphs and copies of manuscripts. Their task over the past several months had been to count the number of letters per word of plays by William Shakespeare, Francis Bacon, Ben Jonson, Christopher Marlowe and other playwrights of the English Renaissance. Their goal, assigned to them by Dr. Thomas Corben Mendenhall, was to prove that Francis Bacon had written the works known to the world as William Shakespeare's. Dr. Mendenhall, a geologist by vocation and stylistic linguist by avocation, had devised a method to identify writers by studying the word length used by each writer. By counting each letter of each word by each writer, individual characteristics emerge, thereby identifying each writer with his own particular style. The theory was that no two writers possessed the same exact writing style, unless it was the same person writing under two different names. Dr. Mendenhall has been approached by Mr. Augustus Hemingway of Boston to prove that Francis Bacon, not Shakespeare, had written the world's most famous plays.

Mrs. Richard Mitchell and Miss Amy Whitman had already been at their task for five hours that day, and they were feeling the strain. Their eyes and backs ached, but they knew their task was almost complete. They had counted thousands of words of dozens of plays of many authors and had diligently recorded their findings on the graphs. The women had completed graphs on Cervantes, Dumas, Dickens, Ben Jonson, Christopher Marlowe, Beaumont and Fletcher, and of course, Francis Bacon and William Shakespeare. The women were excited because Dr. Mendenhall was going to publish their findings in the *Popular Science Monthly* and promised to mention their names.

The graphs varied in appearance. Most authors' graphs peaked at three-letter words, some at two, with the notable exception of Shakespeare, who used words of four letters most frequently. The women were not surprised – of course the world's greatest writer would use more complex words than any other writer in history. However, they had already made a disappointing discovery. Following Dr. Mendenhall's theory, Francis Bacon did not write the plays attributed to Shakespeare. The word lengths did not match up.

But today, as Mrs. Mitchell and Miss Whitman started plotting the graph of Christopher Marlowe's word lengths, the women felt a sense of unease. As the day progressed, they noted a similarity to another author, none other than Shakespeare himself. Marlowe had used the same pattern of words as Shakespeare. In fact, the two graphs were almost identical.

Miss Whitman looked up at Mrs. Mitchell. "I don't understand. Didn't Christopher Marlowe die in 1593?"

"I thought so. Wasn't it a fight about money?"

"How in the world could their graphs be identical? When all the other authors have been so

160

distinctive? I could give you the name of any playwright, just by looking at his graph. How are we going to tell Dr. Mendenhall that his theory is wrong, that different people can write exactly the same way?"

Miss Whitman was devastated. "We've worked so hard, all these months. How can we be taken seriously, if we tell the world all writers have a particular writing style except William Shakespeare, the world's greatest playwright, and Christopher Marlowe, a brawler who got himself killed, whose styles are so similar that they cannot be distinguished?"

Just then, the door to the room opened and Dr. Mendenhall himself walked in. He had taken rather well the news that the study could not support the theory that Bacon had written the works of Shakespeare. After all, he himself did not care who wrote the plays – he was more interested in proving that his scientific method worked. The women's most recent discovery would be a blow.

"Well, ladies, how goes it? Are you just about wrapped up? Any new discoveries today?"

Mrs. Mitchell and Miss Whitman looked at each other nervously. Mrs. Mitchell cleared her throat and Miss Whitman looked down at the table.

"Well, as a matter of fact, Dr. Mendenhall, we have discovered something today, something rather unusual."

"Wonderful," boomed Dr. Mendenhall. "What it is?"

"Well," Mrs. Mitchell cleared her throat again, "I'm not sure that you will be pleased. You see, we have created two graphs by two different authors that appear to be identical."

Dr. Mendenhall frowned. "But that's impossible. All the graphs must be different, significantly different. That's the whole point of the study. Now, after all these months, you're saying that two authors have the identical graphs? Who are they?"

"Well," Mrs. Mitchell said for the third time, "one of the authors is Christopher Marlowe."

"Interesting. He wrote some marvelous plays. Didn't he die young, something about a fight?"

"Yes." Miss Whitman finally found her voice. She had been intrigued by Marlowe's story. As a student of English Renaissance playwrights, Miss Whitman had read many of Marlowe's plays and also accounts of his life and death. "Yes, he was killed in Deptford, in 1593, in a fight with a serving man. Apparently they liked the same woman."

Dr. Mendenhall snorted. "What a waste. I wonder what would have happened had he lived. Some people say his plays are as good as Shakespeare's, if not better. He most likely would have given Shakespeare a run for his money, had he lived."

He paused a moment, considering the possibilities. Then he asked, "So who was the other author?"

Mrs. Mitchell and Miss Whitman looked at each other again, neither one wanting to speak. Finally, Mrs. Mitchell looked Dr. Mendenhall in the eye and said, "William Shakespeare."

Dr. Mendenhall looked thunderstruck. "Do you mean to tell me that not only has my theory about characteristic writing styles been disproved, but that it has been disproved by the world's greatest known writer and some nobody? (Dr. Mendenhall, in his distress over his defunct study, immediately forgot his praise of Marlowe only moments before.)

"I'm sorry, Dr. Mendenhall, but that's what we discovered. We used the exact methodology that we used on all the other authors, on all the other plays. We did nothing differently. See for yourself."

Mrs. Mitchell handed the two graphs to Dr. Mendenhall, who studied them for a moment. Then, his shoulders sagged and he drew a breath. "Well, that's that. I was wrong. Two people *can* have the same exact writing style. If Marlowe hadn't been killed, I would swear on a stack of Bibles that Marlowe and Shakespeare were the same person. My gut tells me I'm right, but the facts tell me I'm wrong. And as I am a man of science, I must concede to the facts."

He dropped the graphs on the table. "Ladies, I thank you for all your hard work over these past months. I know it was a difficult job, and you both fulfilled it perfectly. As disappointed as I am, I have no doubt that your findings are correct, and that the fault lies with the theory. Please finish the study and put the completed graphs on my desk. I'll need them for my article."

"But Dr. Mendenhall, you aren't still going to write the article for *Popular Science*, are you?

"I have to. I've already submitted a synopsis and it's been accepted. The article will be coming out in the December issue. But not with the results I expected."

Miss Whitman had tears in her eyes. "I'm so sorry, Dr. Mendenhall. I wish we could have given you what you had hoped for."

"Thank you, my dear. It would have been thrilling to have proven to the world that Sir Francis

Bacon wrote Shakespeare. God knows enough people believe it. But to prove that a dead man wrote the plays of William Shakespeare? That no one will believe."

He turned, left the room and closed the door.

~ FINIS ~

Dear Reader,

Are you convinced? Has the argument made up your mind? Do you agree that Christopher Marlowe was much more likely to have written the plays than William Shakespeare, based on the historical evidence presented? Do you still have questions, such as "How was the secret kept during Marlowe's lifetime?"

The same type of cover-up occurred in more recent history. During the 1950s, when Senator Joseph McCarthy was hunting Communists in America, many writers were accused and banned from working in Hollywood. In desperation they turned to ghostwriting - producing work under another person's name. The true identity of these writers only came to light within the past decade or so. Desperate times call for desperate measures.

If you still have questions, do some research. There is a lot of material out there about the authorship question.

You may ask yourself, "What does it matter who wrote the plays? It was 400 years ago." The answer is simple – literary justice. The true author of these historical plays deserves to be recognized, even after all these years. 2016 marks the 400th anniversary of the death of William Shakespeare. Isn't it time to put him to rest, once and for all?

MLO

FURTHER READING

Honan, Park. *Christopher Marlowe: Poet and Spy.* Oxford: Oxford University Press, 2005.

Hotson, Leslie. *The Death of Christopher Marlowe.* London: Nonesuch Press, 1925.

Michell, John. *Who Wrote Shakespeare?* London: Thames and Hudson, 1996.

Nichols, Charles. *The Reckoning.* New York: Harcourt Brace and Company, 1992.

Pinksen, Daryl. *Marlowe's Ghost: The Blacklisting of the Man Who Was Shakespeare.* New York: iUniverse, 2008.

Riggs, David. *The World of Christopher Marlowe.* New York: Henry Holt and Company, 2004.

Romany, Frank and Robert Lindsey, eds. *Christopher Marlowe: The Complete Plays.* London: Penguin Books, 2003.

Rowse, A. L. *Christopher Marlowe: His Life and Work.* New York: Harper and Row, 1964.

William Shakespeare: A Biography. New York: Harper and Row, 1963.

Rubbo, Michael. *Much Ado About Something,* Frontline Documentary, 1999.

Shakespeare, William, *The Riverside Shakespeare*. ed. G. Blakemore Evans. Boston: Houghton Mifflin Company, 1974.

The Sonnets. In *The Riverside Shakespeare*, ed. G. Blakemore Evans Boston: Houghton Mifflin, 1974.

Wraight, A.D. *Shakespeare: New Evidence*. London: Adam Hart, 1996.

The Story That the Sonnets Tell. London: Adam Hart Ltd, 1994.

Wraight, A.D., and Virginia F. Stern. *In Search of Christopher Marlowe*. London: The Vanguard Press, Inc., 1965.

NOTES

[i] Public Record Office PC2/14/381
Letter from the Privy Council to the headmaster of
Corpus Christi College, Cambridge, ordering the college
to grant Marlowe his master's degree because Marlowe
had done the queen "good service."

[ii] Public Record Office SP 84/44/60
Robert Sidney's letter from the Lowlands to William
Cecil, Lord Burghley
26 January 1591

Right Honorable
Besides the prisoner Evan Flud, I have also given in charge to
this bearer my anciant twoe other prisoners, the one named
Christofer Marly, by his profession a scholer, and the other
Gifford Gilbert a goldsmith taken heer for coining, and their
mony I have sent over unto yowr Lordship: The matter was
revealed unto me the day after it was done, by one Richard Baines
whome also my Anciant shal bring unto yowr Lordship: He was
theyr chamber fellow and fearing the succes, made me acquainted
with all. The men being examined apart never denied anything,
onely protesting that what was done was onely to se the
Goldsmiths conning: and truly I ame of opinion that the poore
man was onely browght in under that couler, what ever intent the
other twoe had at that time. And indeed they do one accuse
another to have bin the inducers of him, and to have intended to
practis yt heerafter: and have as it were iustified him unto me. But
howsoever it hapned a dutch shilling was uttred, and els not any
peece: and indeed I do not thinck that they wold have uttred many
of them: for the mettal is plain peuter and with half an ey to be
discovered. Notwithstanding I thowght it fitt to send them over

unto yowr Lordship to take theyr trial as yow shal thinck best.
For I wil not stretch my commission to deale in such matters, and
much less to put them at liberty and to deliver them into the towns
hands being the Queens subiects, and not required neyther of this
sayd town I knowe not how it would have bin liked, especially
since part of that which they did counterfet was Her Majesty's
coine. The Goldsmith is an eccellent worckman and if I should
speake my conscience had no intent heerunto. The scholer sais
himself to be very wel known both to the Earle of
Northumberland and my lord Strang. Bains and he do also
accuse one another of intent to goe to the Ennemy or to Rome,
both as they say of malice one to another. Heerof I thowght fitt to
advertis yowr Lordship leaving the rest to their own confession and
my Anciants report. And so do humbly take my leave at
Flushing the 26 of January 1591 [1592 according to our
calendar]
Yowr honors very obedient to do yow service
 R. Sydney
Addressed: *To the right honorable my lord of Burghley Lord*
Treasurer of England.

iii *Greenes, Groats-worth of Witte, bought with a million of*
Repentance (1592)
Booklet written as a moralistic tale, believed to be
autobiographical. Characters introduce songs, fables
and, most notably for our purposes, criticism of actors
and playwrights.

[excerpt]…*Wonder not (for with thee will I first begin), thou*
famous gracer of tragedians, that Greene, who hath said with thee,
like the fool in his heart, There is no God, should now give glory
unto His greatness: for penetrating is His power, His hand lies
heavy upon me, He hath spoken unto me with a voice of thunder,

and I have felt He is a God that can punish enemies. Why should thy excellent wit, His gift, be so blinded, that thou shouldst give no glory to the Giver? Is it pestilent Machiavellian policy that thou hast studied? O peevish folly! What are his rules but mere confused mockeries, able to extirpate in small time the generation of mankind! For if Sic volo, sic jubeo, hold in those that are able to command, and if it be lawful fas et nefas to do anything that is beneficial: only tyrants should possess the earth, and they, striving to exceed in tyranny, should each to other be a slaughter-man; till the mightiest outliving all, one stroke were left for Death, that in one age man's life should end. The brother of this diabolical atheism is dead, and in his life had never the felicity he aimed at; but as he began in craft, lived in fear, and ended in despair....

...And thou, no less deserving than the other two, in some things rarer, in nothing inferior; driven (as myself) to extreme shifts, a little have I to say to thee; and were it not an idolatrous oath, I would swear by sweet St. George, thou art unworthy better hap, sith thou dependest on so mean a stay. Base-minded men all three of you, if by my misery ye be not warned; for unto none of you (like me) sought those burs to cleave,-- those puppets, I mean,-- that speak from our mouths,-- those antics garnished in our colours. Is it not strange that I, to whom they all have been beholden,--is it not like that you, to whom they all have been beholden,-- shall (were ye in that case that I am now) be both at once of them forsaken? Yes, trust them not: for there is an upstart crow, beautified with our feathers, that with his tiger's heart wrapt in a player's hide, supposes he is as well able to bombast out a blank-verse as the best of you: and being an absolute Johannes factotum, is in his own conceit the only Shakescene in a country. Oh, that I might entreat your rare wits to be employed in more profitable courses, and let those apes imitate your past excellence, and never more acquaint them with your admired inventions! I

170

know the best husband of you all will never prove an usurer, and
the kindest of them all will never prove a kind nurse: yet, whilst
you may, seek you better masters; for it is pity men of such rare
wits should be subject to the pleasures of such rude grooms....

^{iv} British Library, MS.Don.d.152 f.4v
Dutch Church Libel, found affixed to the door of the
church where many Protestant immigrants from the
Lowlands worshipped. Because Queen Elizabeth was
their protector, a threat against the immigrants was a
threat against the queen, punishable by death.

Ye strangers y^t doe inhabite in this lande
Note this same writing doe it vnderstand
Conceit it well for savegard of your lyves
Your goods, your children, & your dearest wives
Your Machiavelliun Marchant spoyles the state,
  Your vsery doth leave vs all for deade
Your Artifex, & craftesman works our fate,
And like the Jewes, you eate us vp as bread
The Marchant doth ingross all kinde of wares
  Forestall's the markets, whereso 'ere he goe's
Sends forth his wares, by Pedlers to the faires,
  Retayle's at home, & with his horrible showes: Vndoeth
thowsands
In Baskets your wares trott up & downe
  Carried the streets by the country nation,
You are intelligencers to the state & crowne
  And in your hartes doe wish an alteracion,
You transport goods, & bring vs gawds good store
  Our Leade, our Vittaile, our Ordenance & what nott
That Egipts plagues, vext not the Egyptians more
  Then you doe vs; then death shall be your lotte

171

Noe prize comes in but you make claime therto
    And every merchant hath three trades at least,
And Cutthrote like in selling you vndoe
    vs all, & with our store continually you feast: We cannot
suffer long.
Our pore artificers doe starve & dye
    For y' they cannot now be sett on worke
And for your worke more curious to the ey[.]
    In Chambers, twenty in one house will lurke,
Raysing of rents, was never knowne before
    Living farre better then at native home
And our pore soules, are cleane thrust out of dore
    And to the warres are sent abroade to rome,
To fight it out for Fraunce & Belgia,
    And dy like dogges as sacrifice for you
Expect you therefore such a fatall day
    Shortly on you, & yours for to ensewe: as never was seene.
Since words nor threates nor any other thinge
    canne make you to avoyd this certaine ill
Weele cutte your throtes, in your temples praying
    Not paris massacre so much blood did spill
As we will doe iust vengeance on you all
    In counterfeitinge religion for your flight
When 't'is well knowne, you are loth, for to be thrall
    your coyne, & you as countryes cause to f(s?)light
With Spanish gold, you all are infected
    And with y' gould our Nobles wink at feats
Nobles said I? nay men to be reiected,
    Upstarts yt enioy the noblest seates
That wound their Countries brest, for lucres sake
    And wrong our gracious Queene & Subiects good
By letting strangers make our harts to ake
    For which our swords are whet, to shedd their blood

172

And for a truth let it be vnderstoode/   Fly, Flye, & never
returne.
per. Tam-berlaine

^v Bodleian Library, MS.Don.d.152 f.4v
Letter from the Star Chamber authorizing search,
seizure and torture of those responsible, or even
suspected, of being connected with the threats against
Protestant immigrants.

^{vi} British Museum, Harl. MS., 6848 f. 188.9.
Statement of Thomas Kyd while under torture at
Bridwell Prison, stating that the "heretical" treatise on
Unitarianism found in Kyd's room belonged to
Christopher Marlowe, effectively accusing Marlowe of
being a heretic.

^{vii} Privy Council entry 18 May 1593

^{viii} Privy Council entry 20 May 1593

^{ix} Bodleian Library Harley MS.6848 ff.185-6
The Baines Note, with additions and deletions by
person(s) unknown.

A note contaynineg the opinion of one Christopher Marley
concernyge his damnable opinion and Iudgment of Religioun, and
scorn of gods worde.

[Written after CM's death]
A note delivred on whitsun eve last of the most horrible
blasphemes and damnable opinions utteryd of xtofer MArly who
since whitsonday dyed a sodden & violent deathe.

[Written after first addition]
...who within iij days after came to a sodden & fearfull end of his life.

That the Indians and many Authors of antiquity haue assuredly writen aboue 16 thousand yeares agone wher as Adam is proued to haue lived within 6 thowsand yeares.

He affirmeth that Moyses was but a Jugler, & that one Heriots being Sir W Raleighs man can do more then he.

That Moyses made the Jewes to travell xl yeares in the wildernes, (which Jorney might haue bin Done in lesse then one yeare) ere they Came to the promised land, to thintent that those who were privy to most of his subtilties might perish and so an everlasting superstition Remain in the harts of the people.

That the first beginning of Religioun was only to keep men in awe.

That it was an easy matter for Moyses being brought vp in all the artes of the Egiptians to abuse the Jewes being a rude & grosse people.

That Christ was a bastard and his mother dishonest.

That he was the sonne of a Carpenter, and that if the Jewes among whome he was borne did Crucify him theie best knew him and whence he Came.

That Crist deserved better to Dy then Barrabas and that the
Jewes made a good Choise, though Barrabas were both a thief and
murtherer.

That if there be any god or any good Religion, then it is in the
papistes because the service of god is performed with more
Cerimonies, as Elevation of the mass, organs, singing men,
Shaven Crownes & cetera. That all protestants are Hypocriticall
asses.

That if he were put to write a new Religion, he would vndertake
both a more Exellent and Admirable methode and that all the
new testament is filthily written.

That the woman of Samaria & her sister were whores & that
Christ knew them dishonestly.

That St John the Evangelist was bedfellow to Christ and leaned
alwaies in his bosome, that he vsed him as the sinners of Sodoma.

That all they that loue not Tobacco & Boies were fooles.

That all the apostles were fishermen and base fellowes neyther of
wit nor worth, that Paull only had wit but he was a timerous
fellow in bidding men to be subiect to magistrates against his
Conscience.

That he had as good Right to Coine as the Queene of England,
and that he was acquainted with one poole a prisoner in newgate
who hath greate Skill in mix=ture of mettals and hauing learned
some things of him he ment through help of a Cunninge stamp
maker to Coin French Crownes pistolets and Eng=lish
shillinges.

175

That if Christ would haue instituted the sacrament with more Ceremoniall Reverence it would haue bin had in more admiration, that it would haue bin much better being administred in a Tobacco pipe.

That the Angell Gabriell was Baud to the holy ghost, because he brought the salutation to Mary.

That one Ric Cholmley hath Confessed that he was persuaded by Marloe's Reasons to become an Atheist.

~~These thinges, with many other shall by good & honest witnes be aproved to be his opinions and Comon Speeches, and that this Marlow doth not only hould them himself, but almost into every Company he Cometh he perswades men to Atheism willing them not to be afeard of bugbeares and hobgoblins, and vtterly scorning both god and his ministers as I Richard Baines will Justify & approue both by mine oth and the testimony of many honest men, and almost al men with whome he hath Conversed any time will testify the same, and as I think all men in Cristianity ought to indevor that the mouth of so dangerous a member may be stopped, he saith likewise that he hath quoted a number of Contrarieties oute of the Scripture which he hath giuen to some great men who in Convenient time shalbe named. When these thinges shalbe Called in question the witnes shalbe produced.~~

Richard Baines

ˣBodleian Library Harley MS.6848 f.190
Remembraunces of wordes & matters against Ric Cholmeley.

That hee speaketh in generall all evill of the Counsell; sayenge that they are all Atheistes & Machiavillians, especially my Lord Admirall

That hee made certen libellious verses in Commendacen of papistes & Seminary priestes very greately inveighinge againste the State, amonge which lynes this
was one, Nor may the Prince deny the Papall Crowne

That hee had a certen booke (as hee saieth) deliverd him by Sir Robert Cecill of whom hee geveth very scandalous reporte, that hee should invite him
to consider thereof & to frame verses & libells in Commendacen of constant Priests & vertuous Recusants, this booke is in Custodie & is called an
Epistle of Comforte & is printed at Paris.

That he railes at Mr Topcliffe & hath written another libell Joyntlye against Sir Francis Drake & Justice younge whom hee saieth hee will Couple vp together because hee hateth them alike

That when the muteny happened after the Portingale voyage in the Strand hee said that hee repented him of nothinge more then that hee had not killed my Lord Threasorer with his owne handes sayenge that hee could not have done god better service, this was spoken in the hearinge of Franncis Clerke & many other Souldieres

That hee saieth hee doeth entirely hate the Lord Chamberleyn & hath good cause so to doe.

That he saieth & verely beleveth that one Marlowe is able to showe more sounde reasons for Atheisme then any devine in Englande is able to geve to prove devinitie & that Marloe tolde him that hee hath read the Atheist lecture to Sir walter Raliegh & others.

That he saieth that hee hath certen men corrupted by his persuasions, who wilbee ready at all tymes & for all causes to sweare whatsoever seemeth good to him, Amonge whom is one Henry younge & Jasper Borage & others

That hee so highly esteemeth his owne witt & Judgement that hee saieth that noman are sooner devyned & abused then the Counsell themselves

That hee can goe beyonde & Cosen them as hee liste & that if hee make any Complainte in behalfe of the Queene hee shall not onely bee privately heard & enterteyned, but hee will so vrge the Counsell for money that without hee have what hee liste hee will doe nothinge

That beinge imployed by some of her majestys prevy Counsaile for the apprehension of Papists & other dangerous men hee vsed he saieth to take money of them & would lett them passe in spighte of the Counsell.

That he saieth that william Parry was hanged drawen & quartered but in Jeste that hee was a grosse Asse overreached by Cunninge, & that in trueth hee now meante to kill the Queene more then himselfe had.

xi "Protestation," the seventh of the so-called Mar-prelate Tracts, a series of illegal pamphlets printed by John Penry in 1588-89. The tracts were puritanical attacks on the Anglican Church in general and Archbishop Whitgift in particular.

xii Pro Chancery C260/174/27
Found and translated from Latin by Leslie Hotson in his 1925 book *The Death of Christopher Marlowe*.

KENT / INQUISITION Indented taken at Detford Strand in the aforesaid County of Kent within the verge on the first day of June in the year of the reign of Elizabeth by the grace of God of England France and Ireland Queen defender of the faith &c thirtyfifth, in the presence of William Danby, Gentleman, Coroner of the household of our said lady the Queen, upon view of the body of Christopher Morley, there lying dead & slain, upon oath of Nicholas Draper, Gentleman, Wolstan Randall, gentleman, William Curry, Adrian Walker, John Barber, Robert Baldwyn, Giles ffeld, George Halfepenny, Henry Awger, James Batt, Henry Bendyn, Thomas Batt senior, John Baldwyn, Alexander Burrage, Edmund Goodcheepe, & Henry Dabyns who say [upon] their oath that Ingram ffrysar, late of London, Gentleman, and the aforesaid Christopher Morley, and Nicholas Skeres, late of London, Gentleman, and Robert Poley of London aforesaid, Gentleman, on the thirtieth of May in the aforesaid thirtyfifth year, at the aforesaid Detford Strand in the aforesaid County of Kent within the verge about the tenth hour before noon of the same day met together in a room in the house of a certain Eleanor Bull, widow; & there passed the time together & dined & after dinner were in quiet sort together & walked in the garden belonging to the said house until the sixth hour after noon of the same day & then returned from the said garden to the room

179

aforesaid & there together and in company supped; & after
supper the said Ingram & Christopher Morley were in speech &
uttered one to the other divers malicious words for the reason that
they could not be at one nor agree about the payment of the sum of
pence, that is, le recknynge, there; & the said Christopher Morley
then lying upon a bed in the room where they supped, & moved
with anger against the said Ingram ffrysar upon the words
aforesaid spoken between them, and the said Ingram then &
there sitting in the room aforesaid with his back towards the bed
where the said Christopher Morley was then lying, sitting near the
bed, that is, nere the bed, & with the front part of his body
towards the table & the aforesaid Nicholas Skeres & Robert
Poley sitting on either side of the said Ingram in such a manner
that the same Ingram ffrysar in no wise could take flight; it so
befell that the said Christopher Morley on a sudden & of his
malice towards the said Ingram aforethought, then & there
maliciously drew the dagger of the said Ingram which was at his
back, and with the same dagger the said Christopher Morley then
& there maliciously gave the aforesaid Ingram two wounds on his
head of the length of two inches & of the depth of a quarter of an
inch; whereupon the said Ingram, in fear of being slain, & sitting
in the manner aforesaid between the said Nicholas Skeres &
Robert Poley so that he could not in any wise get away, in his own
defence & for the saving of his life, then & there struggled with
the said Christopher Morley to get back from him his dagger
aforesaid; in which affray the same Ingram could not get away
from the said Christopher Morley; and so it befell in that affray
that the said Ingram, in defence of his life, with the dagger
aforesaid to the value of 12d, gave the said Christopher then &
there a mortal wound over his right eye of the depth of two inches
& of the width of one inch; of which mortal wound the aforesaid
Christopher Morley then & there instantly died; And so the
Jurors aforesaid say upon their oath that the said Ingram killed

& slew Christopher Morley aforesaid on the thirtieth day of May in the thirtyfifth year named above at Detford Strand aforesaid within the verge in the room aforesaid within the verge in the manner and form aforesaid in the defence and saving of his own life, against the peace of our said lady the Queen, her now crown & dignity; And further the said Jurors say upon their oath that the said Ingram after the slaying aforesaid perpetrated & done by him in the manner & form aforesaid neither fled nor withdrew himself; But what goods or chattels, lands or tenements the said Ingram had at the time of the slaying aforesaid, done & perpetrated by him in the manner & form aforesaid, the said Jurors are totally ignorant. In witness of which thing the said Coroner as well as the Jurors aforesaid to this Inquisition have interchangeably set their seals. Given the day & year above named &c.

by WILLIAM DANBY Coroner

[xiii] Chancery Miscellanea, Bundle 34, File 8, No. 241a

[xiv] Patent Rolls 1401, 33, 34. Ingram Frizer's Pardon. Translated by Leslie Hotson in his book *The Death of Christopher Marlowe.*

"From the Queen to all her officers and loyal subjects etc., greetings. By means of a certain Inquisition indented taken at Detford Strand in our County of Kent within the verge on the first day of last June aforesaid in the presence of William Danby, Gentleman, Coroner of the household of our household, upon view of the body of Christopher Morley, there lying dead & slain, upon oath of Nicholas Draper, Gentleman, Wolstan Randall, gentleman, William Curry, Adrian Walker, John Barber, Robert Baldwin, Giles ffeld, George Halfepenny, Henry Awger,

181

James Batt, Henry Bendin, Thomas Batt senior, John Baldwyn, Alexander Burrage, Edmund Goodcheepe, & Henry Dabyns who said upon oath that Ingram ffrysar, late of London, Gentleman, and the aforesaid Christopher Morley, and Nicholas Skeres, late of London, Gentleman, and Robert Poley of London aforesaid, Gentleman, on the thirtieth of May last aforesaid, at the aforesaid Detford Strand in our aforesaid County of Kent within the verge about the tenth hour before noon of the same day met together in a room in the house of a certain Eleanor Bull, widow; & there passed the time together & dined & after dinner were in quiet sort together & walked in the garden belonging to the said house until the sixth hour after noon of the same day & then returned from the said garden to the room aforesaid & there together and in company supped; & after supper the said Ingram & Christopher Morley were in speech & uttered one to the other divers malicious words for the reason that they could not be at one nor agree about the payment of the sum of pence, that is, le Reckoninge, there; & the said Christopher Morley then lying upon a bed in the room where they supped, & moved with anger against the said Ingram ffrysar upon the words aforesaid spoken between them, and the said Ingram then & there sitting in the room aforesaid with his back towards the bed where the said Christopher Morley was then lying, sitting near the bed, that is, nere the Bedd, & with the front part of his body towards the table & the aforesaid Nicholas Skeres & Robert Poley sitting on either side of the said Ingram in such a manner that the same Ingram ffrysar in no wise could take flight; it so befell that the said Christopher Morley on a sudden & of his malice towards the said Ingram aforethought, then & there maliciously drew the dagger of the said Ingram which was at his back, and with the same dagger the said Christopher Morley then & there maliciously gave the aforesaid Ingram two wounds on his head of the length of two inches & of the depth of a quarter of an inch;

whereupon the said Ingram, in fear of being slain, & sitting in
the manner aforesaid between the said Nicholas Skeres & Robert
Poley so that he could not in any wise get away, in his own defence
& for the saving of his life, then & there struggled with the said
Christopher Morley to get back from him his dagger aforesaid; in
which affray the same Ingram could not get away from the said
Christopher Morley; and so it befell in that affray that the said
Ingram, in defence of his life, with the dagger aforesaid to the
value of twelve pence, gave the said Christopher then & there a
mortal wound over his right eye of the depth of two inches & of
the width of one inch; of which mortal wound the aforesaid
Christopher Morley then & there instantly died. And so that the
said Ingram killed & slew Christopher Morley aforesaid on the
thirtieth day of last May aforesaid at Detford Strande aforesaid
in our said County of Kent within the verge in the room aforesaid
within the verge in the manner & form aforesaid in the defence
and saving of his own life against our peace our crown & dignity.
As more fully appears by the tenor of the Record of the
Inquisition aforesaid which we caused to come before us in our
Chancery by virtue of our writ. We therefore moved by piety have
pardoned the same Ingram ffrisar the breach of our peace which
pertains to us against the said Ingram for the death above
mentioned & grant to him our firm peace. Provided nevertheless
that the right remain in our Court if anyone should wish to
complain of him concerning the death above mentioned In
testimony &c Witness the Queen at Kewe on the 28th day of
June."

XV Dedication of *Venus and Adonis*

To the Right Honorable Henrie Wriothesley, Earle of
Southampton, and Baron of Tichfield.

183

Right Honourable, I know not how I shall offend in dedicating my unpolisht lines to your Lordship, nor how the worlde will censure mee for choosing so strong a proppe to support so weake a burthen, onelye if your Honour seeme but pleased, I account my selfe highly praised, and vowe to take advantage of all idle houres, till I have honoured you with some graver labour. But if the first heire of my invention prove deformed, I shall be sorie it had so noble a god-father: and never after eare so barren a land, for feare it yeeld me still so bad a harvest, I leave it to your Honourable survey, and your Honor to your hearts content, which I wish may alwaies answere your owne wish, and the worlds hopefull expectation.

Your Honors in all dutie,
William Shakespeare

xvi Dozens of "parallelisms" can be found in Calvin Hoffman's 1955 book *The Murder of the Man Who Was Shakespeare*.

xvii Thomas Beard, *The Theatre of God's Judgment*, 1598. Beard was a Puritan who believed that Marlowe's violent death was God's punishment of playwrights and the theatre.

[excerpt]…*Not inferior to any of the former in atheism and impiety, and equal to all in manner of punishment was one of our own nation, of fresh and late memory, called Marlin by profession a scholar, brought up from his youth in the University of Cambridge, but by practice a play-maker, and a poet of scurrility, who by giving too large a swinge to his own wit, and suffering his lust to have the full reins, fell (not without just desert) to the outrage and extremity that he denied God and his son Christ, and not only in word blasphemed the Trinity, but also (as it is*

credibly reported) wrote books against it, affirming our Savior to be but a deceiver, and Moses to be but a conjurer and seducer of the people, and the Holy Bible to be but vain and idle stories, and all religion but vain and idle policy.

But see what a hook the Lord put in the nostrils of this barking dog. It so fell out that in London streets as he purposed to stab one whom he owed a grudge unto with his dagger, the other party perceiving so avoided the stroke, that withal catching hold of his wrist, he stabbed his own dagger into his own head, in such sort that notwithstanding all the means of surgery that could be wrought, he shortly after died thereof. The manner of his death being so terrible (for he even cursed and blasphemed to his last gasp, and together with his breath an oath flew out of his mouth) that it was not only a manifest sign of God's judgment, but also an horrible and fearful terror to all that beheld him. But herein did the justice of God most notably appear, in that he compelled his own hand which had written those blasphemies to be the instrument to punish him, and that in his brain, which had devised the same....

xviii Francis Meres, *Palladis Tamia. Wits Treasury.* Printed by P. Short for Cuthbert Burbie. 1598.

xix Dedication of "Hero and Leander," 1598, published by Edward Blount with Marlowe's two stanzas.

To the Right Worshipfull, Sir Thomas Walsingham, Knight
Sir, wee thinke not our selves discharged of the dutie wee owe to our friend, when wee have brought the breathlesse bodie to the earth: for albeit the eye there taketh his ever farwell of that beloved object, yet the impression of the man, that hath beene deare unto us, living an after life in our memory, there putteth us in mind of

farther obsequies due unto the deceased. And namely of the performance of whatsoever we may judge shal make to his living credit, and to the effecting of his determinations prevented by the stroke of death. By these meditations (as by an intellectuall will) I suppose my selfe executor to the unhappily deceased author of this Poem, upon who knowing that in his lift time you bestowed many kind favours, entertaining the parts of reckoning and woorth which you found in him, with good countenance and liberall affection: I cannot but see so far into the will of him dead, but what- soever issue of his brain should chance to come abroad, that the first

breath it should take might be the gentle aire of your liking: for since his selfe had ben accustomed therunto, it would proove more agreeable and thriving to his right children, than any other foster countenance whatsoever. At this time seeing that this unfinished Tragedy happens under my hands to be imprinted; of a double duty, the one to your selfe, the other to the deceased, I present the same to your most favourable allowance, offring my utmost selfe now and ever to bee readie,
At your Worships disposing:
Edward Blunt.

[xx] "The Passionate Shepherd to His Love"
by Christopher Marlowe

Come live with me and be my love,
And we will all the pleasures prove,
That Valleys, groves, hills, and fields,
Woods, or steepy mountain yields.

And we will sit upon the Rocks,
Seeing the Shepherds feed their flocks,
By shallow Rivers to whose falls

Melodious birds sing Madrigals.

And I will make thee beds of Roses
And a thousand fragrant posies,
A cap of flowers, and a kirtle
Embroidered all with leaves of Myrtle;

A gown made of the finest wool
Which from our pretty Lambs we pull;
Fair lined slippers for the cold,
With buckles of the purest gold;

A belt of straw and Ivy buds,
With Coral clasps and Amber studs:
And if these pleasures may thee move,
Come live with me, and be my love.

The Shepherds' Swains shall dance and sing
For thy delight each May-morning:
If these delights thy mind may move,
Then live with me, and be my love.

xxi "Nymph's Reply to the Shepherd"
attributed to Sir Walter Ralegh

If all the world and love were young,
And truth in every Shepherd's tongue,
These pretty pleasures might me move,
To live with thee, and be thy love.

Time drives the flocks from field to fold,
When Rivers rage and Rocks grow cold,
And Philomel becometh dumb,

The rest complains of cares to come.

The flowers do fade, and wanton fields,
To wayward winter reckoning yields,
A honey tongue, a heart of gall,
Is fancy's spring, but sorrow's fall.

Thy gowns, thy shoes, thy beds of Roses,
Thy cap, thy kirtle, and thy posies
Soon break, soon wither, soon forgotten:
In folly ripe, in reason rotten.

Thy belt of straw and Ivy buds,
The Coral clasps and amber studs,
All these in me no means can move
To come to thee and be thy love.

But could youth last, and love still breed,
Had joys no date, nor age no need,
Then these delights my mind might move
To live with thee, and be thy love.

xxii Thomas Thorpe's dedicatory letter to Edward
Blount, in *The First Book of Lucan*, 1600.

To his Kind and True Friend:
Edward Blount

Blount: I purpose to be blunt with you, and out of my dullnesse to
encounter you with a Dedication in the memory of that pure
Elementall wit, Chr. Marlow; whose ghoast or Genius is to be
seene walke the Churchyard (at the least) three or foure sheets.

Me thinks you should presently looke wilde now, and grow humourously frantique upon the tast of it. Well, least you should, let mee tell you.

This spirit was sometime a familiar of your own. Lucans first booke translated; which (in regard of your old right in it) I have rais'd in the circle of your Patronage. But stay now, Edward (if I mistake not) you are to accommodate your selfe with some fewe instructions, touching the property of a Patron that you are not yet possest of; and to study them for your better grace as our Gallants do fashions. First, you must be proud and thinke you have merit inough in you, though you are ne're so emptie; then when I bring you the booke take physicke. and keepe state, assigne me a time by your man to come againer and afore the day, be sure to have chang'd your lodging; in the meane time sleepe little, and sweat with the invention of some pittiful dry jest or two which you may happen to utter, with some litle (or not at al) marking of your friends when you have found a place for them to come in at; or if by chance something has dropt from you worth the taking up weary all that come to you with the often repetition of it; Censure scorne-fully inough, and somewhat like a travailer: commend nothing least you discredit your (that which you would seeme to have) judgemenl. These things if you can mould your self to them Ned I make no question but they will not become you. One speciall vertue in our Patrons of these daies I have promist my selfe you shall fit excellently, which is to give nothing: Yet, thy love I will challenge as my peculiar Object both in this, and (I hope) manie more succeeding offices: Farewell, I affect not the world should measure my thoughts to thee by a scale of this Nature: leave to thinke good of me when I fall from thee.

Thine in all rites of perfect friendship,
THOM.THORPE

xxiii Ben Jonson, *Every Man Out of His Humour*, 1599. "Not without mustard" is a reference to the motto that appears on John (father of William) Shakespeare's application for a coat-of-arms, which read "Not without right" or "No, without right" depending on interpretation. In 1576, John Shakespeare applied for a family coat-of-arms. He was denied. Twenty years later in 1596, John reapplied, and this time the application was approved, possibly as another carrot for William's cooperation. Jonson's line pokes fun at the Shakespeare application, amusing those in the theatre community who knew that William Shakespeare was an impostor and deserved neither the coat-of-arms nor credit for the plays.

xxiv Dedication page from *The Sonnets*.

TO.THE.ONLIE.BEGETTER.OF.
THESE.INSVING.SONNETS.
Mr.W.H. ALL.HAPPINESSE.
AND.THAT.ETERNITIE.
PROMISED.
BY.
OVR.EVERLIVING.POET.
WISHETH.
THE.WELL-WISHING.
ADVENTURER.IN.
SETTING.
FORTH.

T.T.

[xxv] There are many books and websites devoted to William Shakespeare's will, including a detailed listing of his possessions and what he left to whom. Again, please note, not a single book, not even a Bible, was noted among William Shakespeare's possessions at the time of his death.

[xxvi] Preface to the First Folio, by Ben Jonson.

> *This Figure, that thou here feest put,*
> *It was for gentle Shakespeare cut:*
> *Wherein the Grauer had a strife*
> *with Naure, to out-doo the life:*
> *O, could he but haue dravvne his vvit*
> *As vvell in frasse, as he hath hit*
> *Hisface; the Print vvould then surpasse*
> *All, that vvas euer in frasse.*
> *But, since he cannot, Reader, looke*
> *Not on his picture, but his Booke.*
> *B.I.*

[xxvii] *The Popular Science Monthly*, December 1901.

61818526R00127

Made in the USA
Lexington, KY
21 March 2017